THE WORRY KNOT

Mary Bleckwehl

Immortal Works LLC
1505 Glenrose Drive
Salt Lake City, Utah 84104
Tel: (385) 202-0116

Cover Art by Ashley Literski
http://strangedevotion.wixsite.com/strangedesigns

ISBN 978-1-953491-31-2
ASIN B09NTKHSST

For Bill, our children, and our journey

PROLOGUE

My twin sisters turned me into a worry wart with one simple question. But I don't blame them. They were only four.
~Rourke

On the day of the simple question, Dad was in the basement with a blanket wrapped tight around Carson in an attempt to calm him after Mom accidentally mentioned the S word: *storm.* The mere sight of a cloud or a word about weather always sent Carson whimpering to the basement.

The simple question came from my sister Eva.

"Will Carson always be this way?"

"You mean scared of storms?" Mom replied.

"Yeah, that. And needing somebody to take care of him?"

"Probably."

"Forever?" Lucy stretched the word out long as she leaned forward and peered into Mom's face waiting for an answer.

Tears sprang into Mom's eyes as she choked on her words. "Daddy and I will take care of your brother as long as we can."

"It's okay, Mommy," cooed Eva as she stroked Mom's hand. "Carson can live with Rourke when he grows up. Rourke's good at taking care of him."

The moment Mom nodded in agreement was the moment my stomach turned itself into a knot, because Eva is wrong. I'm not good at taking care of others. I have trouble taking care of myself.

CHAPTER 1

When you're twelve, are you too old to have an imaginary friend?
~Rourke

I lie in my bed staring at the glow-in-the-dark stars on my ceiling and wonder what it will be like to go to the same school as Carson again. Since tomorrow's the first day of middle school for me, I'll soon find out. It shouldn't matter that I have a brother who has trouble fitting in, but it does. I hate it when kids are mean to him and he doesn't even realize it. Mom and Dad expect me to watch out for him, and I want to protect him, but how am I going to guard him from Bart the Bully and all the other middle school awfuls?

Finally, I relax. I'm warm and safe and asleep. Until someone shoves me. Six or seven kids poke and taunt me. I back away. "What's with your brother?" they chant.

"Leave him alone!" I beg. But the gang shoves me closer and closer to the edge of...something. The sound of rushing water gets my heart pumping, and I push against them, fighting to get away.

I fall, jolting awake. My arms and legs thrash around in my blankets, and my heart attempts to leave my chest.

I force my body to use the breathing I learned in boy scouts to calm myself. Breathe in through the nose...out through the mouth. Again. In through the nose. Out through the mouth.

Finally my temples no longer feel like they're ready to explode. But there's something else. No, *someone* else here.

Oh, not again.

Sam's back.

CHAPTER 2

Thank goodness for Rourke's help in getting Carson to school.
~Mrs. Berger

I snap my alarm off at 7:02 a.m. Another night of bad dreams, and another morning of gut ache.

Something wet and slimy licks my arm as it dangles over the edge of my bed. "Good morning, Hank," I mumble. "Where's your twin sister?"

I hear a soft woof and coax my eyes open a sliver to see our two Irish setters staring at me.

I pat their heads and stare out my window in the direction of Hazard Middle School. According to Dad, it's exactly one-point-one miles from our house. If you live more than a mile away, you can ride the bus. But who wants to ride the bus when you're in middle school?

Carson's been riding the short bus there the past two years. It's for kids who don't do well on the regular bus of pranks and flying food. Since I'm attending the same school as Carson this year, Mom insists we walk together.

"The autism specialist wants us to give Carson some independence," Mom told me last night, "so one of his goals this year is to walk to school."

I didn't understand the logic. "Mom, how is walking with me helping Carson gain independence?"

She just rubbed my head and said, "Oh, Rourke. Don't worry. It will be fine."

Fine. My family is all about fine. Except me.

For weeks I'd been telling myself it would be no big deal to be in the same school as Carson again, but after last night's nightmare, I'm not so sure. And if my imaginary friend, Sam, is back, it means my concern over Carson has increased too. The thought pulls at the knot forming in my stomach. The worry knot.

I glance at the clock—7:10. I need to get going. After a quick shower, I lean toward the bathroom mirror. My hair is bleached from the summer sun, and the waves are—well, very wavy. Where does my part look better? I try it on the right. The left. I add water to my comb and push it all straight back. Yikes! I can't look like a goon on my first day. I decide on the left part.

Back in my bedroom, I rummage through my dresser and change from a brown polo shirt to a faded blue tee. Imaginary Sam gives me the thumbs up just before I hear Mom.

"That shirt looks great, Rourke! It matches your eyes."

"Oh, hi, Mom." My face grows warm. "It's a T-shirt. Guys in middle school wear T-shirts."

She tousles my hair and laughs. "Better grab some breakfast. Phinney will be here soon. Come on, Carson. Let's find your other shoe."

Carson is wearing his usual two layers of Superman shirts and carrying his sticker collection box. "D-d-d-oes my shirt match my eyes too, Mom?"

"Absolutely, Carson. You look great!"

As I slip my shoes on, I get an idea and hustle down the stairs with both dogs on my heels.

"Mom, I'm going to be leaving early for school every day so I can get some extra homework time in. Carson can ride the short bus like he did last year."

"Why, Rourke!" Mom hands me a banana and Gatorade along with her proudest-moment smile that makes me all warm inside. "I love the way you're already thinking about your grades!"

"Well, I don't want the teachers to think I'm a slacker or something."

"That's wonderful!" She gives me a mom-hug. I pull away before she gets all mushy. I mean, I'm going into seventh grade.

I twist off the Gatorade cap and take a drink.

"However, you can get up early and do homework here." She glances into the hallway where Carson is struggling with which shoe is left and right.

"But, Mom! What if Carson runs off on the way to school or stops to count the cars on Emerson Street? I'm not his babysitter!"

Mom's eyes widen, and her lips quiver. Too late I realize I was practically yelling and sense Sam urging me to let it go.

"Hey, Berger Brothers!" Phinney calls through the screen door. "Are we ready for the big-time?"

My best friend's arrival ends the chance for me to apologize to Mom, plus Carson scrambles out the door, forcing me to throw my drink into my backpack and take off after him.

"Come on, Phinney. Carson's fast."

"Enjoy your first day of school, boys! Carson, wait at the stop sign for your brother to help you cross."

Running with a backpack full of school supplies isn't easy, and within two blocks, something cold drips down my back.

"Hey! Wait up, Carson! I know you're excited about the first day but we don't need to make this a race!"

Carson flaps his hands and keeps running. "I can't be late. M-m-miss Cynthia will be mad. I can't be late. Miss Cynthia will be m-m-mad."

Phinney and I sprint to catch up.

"You weren't kiddin'. Carson's a rocket!" proclaims Phinney.

"Carson, we're not late. Please! *Stop!*"

"Stop" was apparently the magic word as he came to a halt and waited for us.

Breathing hard, Phinney slaps Carson on the shoulder and laughs. "Man, you should be on the cross-country team with me. You're fast!"

"Fast. Yes, I'm fast." Carson rocks back and forth and looks anxiously toward the school. "Miss Cynthia is waiting. Waiting to see my new sticker collection."

Still trying to catch my breath, I give him a big smile. "Yes, she is. But you have ninth grade legs. As a favor to me and my seventh grade legs, could we walk the rest of the way?"

Carson reluctantly agrees, then reminds me four or five times that, "Miss Cynthia needs to see my stickers."

Two blocks from school I turn to Carson and touch his arm. He flinches as if I just gave him an electric shock.

"Hey, Carson. Remember how Mom says you're supposed to try things on your own?"

He rocks back and forth again and stares at the sidewalk.

"Every day when we get to Emerson Street, you can walk on ahead."

Carson claps in an awkward sort of way and makes a 180-degree turn, enthusiastically marching down the sidewalk as if headed to a national sticker convention. No flapping. No running.

Phinney high-fives me. "Rourke Berger, you win the brother of the year prize!"

Phinney is being sincere, but the butterflies begin to flutter as I watch Carson go. *Maybe I shouldn't let him walk alone. It should be no big deal. Just in case, I'll stay close to be sure he makes it okay.*

As we near the school, the butterflies multiply. Kids pile off buses and move toward the school entrance. With all the foot traffic, I lose sight of Carson for just a second. I scan the crowd. My throat tightens and I have trouble breathing. I exhale with relief as I see him wave at his old bus driver.

"Hi, Mr. Phil!" Carson yells—and bolts in front of a moving bus the size of Texas.

CHAPTER 3

I gasp. My feet are cemented to the sidewalk. *Carson's going to get run over by a bus and die on the first day of school!* I want to die too. My mother will kill me anyway, once she hears I let him walk on ahead by himself.

My chest pounds and I'm back in the same nightmare that's been haunting me all summer. I hang by my fingernails on the cliff edge with dark waters swirling below, only this time I'm not asleep. I sink to my knees on the sidewalk.

Sam screams inside my head to do something, so I do.

"Carson! *Look out!*"

I'm positive the entire middle school universe hears me. But Carson freezes.

Luckily Mr. Phil has been practicing stopping on a dime and misses Carson.

Someone hauls me back from the ledge as I fall forward, holding the sides of my head in my trembling hands. "Thank you, Sam," I whisper.

Phinney gives me a confused look. "What did you just say?"

I shake my head as I return to reality. "Nothing. I'm just...nothing."

I pick myself up from the sidewalk and numbly walk toward the school with the realization that Carson is always one step away from an accident. No matter how I try to relax when I'm with him, I can't. He's my brother, my *only* brother, and I can't let anything happen to him.

And Sam? I shake my head in frustration. I thought he was long gone. I'm almost thirteen. Only little kids have imaginary friends.

When I enter the school, I nearly collide with Peter Salzmann, my redneck neighbor with the monster mutts. *Could my day get any worse?*

"Your brother okay?" He must have witnessed the near-miss bus incident.

"Fine." I mumble my family mantra and head straight to the bathroom to decompress. Standing in one of the stalls, I lean my forehead against the coolness of the metal door. Breathe. My Gatorade-soaked shirt is sticking to my back. Breathe. Carson almost got run over by a bus. I let that sink in. Breathe. This kid is more accident prone than anyone I know.

When I step inside my homeroom, I've suddenly stepped back in time. Miss Thompson stands at the front of the room. The same Miss Thompson who was the social worker I told my deepest secrets to in elementary school. She looks up and smiles at me. My luck just changed! This awesome person is not only my homeroom teacher but my science teacher, which means she's the first and last teacher I'll see every day!

As Miss Thompson begins telling us about our schedule, I close my eyes. Her calm voice explains the ins and outs of seventh grade. I grew to love that voice when I had my one-on-one time with her in fourth grade. I seldom looked at her then either. I just listened. And now, even though she's talking about homework and how to avoid detention, her voice is the next best thing to a hot fudge brownie sundae. I'll want to get to school on time every day just to hear that voice.

Phinney apparently notices me in dreamland. He whispers, "Tell your mom that coming to school early for homework is mandatory."

I smile and settle into my seat. The worry knot in my gut relaxes.

I hate to leave, but there's more to middle school than homeroom. Phinney and I walk to art class where I take a seat across from a girl I don't recognize. *Wait! That's mousy Monica Monahan. Wow! What happened to her over the summer?* In sixth grade she was just a regular girl with a pointy little nose, and now she's—not mousy at all.

Phinney notices her too and fans himself.

Monica turns and catches me staring. My face heats up as I look away, but not before I see her lips curl up. She moves her long tanned legs closer to the aisle and crosses them. How am I going to get a decent grade in here with this distraction? Maybe she'd like to go to the movies with me. Like I'd ever get the nerve to ask.

DURING STUDY HALL I get introduced to the crazy world of hippie-teacher, Mad Marlys. I've heard stories of students being cruel to her and taking advantage of the fact that she's a tad wacky.

Toward the end of study hall, someone's phone rings with an obnoxious foghorn sound. Everyone holds their breath and eyes Mad Marlys to gauge her reaction.

"Everyone out!"

What?

She thinks it's the fire alarm and directs us to evacuate.

Naturally we're the only class standing outdoors, and it doesn't take Mad Marlys long to figure out there's something weird about that. Back inside the classroom I notice her two hearing aids. Ah! The poor lady can't hear.

When study hall ends, kids spill out the door, laughing so hard I'm afraid they'll have some internal injuries. It dawns on me I haven't thought of Sam or Carson for an entire hour. Distractions can be good, but unfortunately this one is at the expense of Mad Marlys's hearing disability.

My stomach growls. Only one more class before lunch, thank goodness!

Math is loaded with guys from my baseball team, including Bart the Bully. Judging from the crowd surrounding his desk when I walk in the room, he's still *numero uno* on the popularity chart. But he's a jerk in my book for how he treated Carson last summer at our first baseball game. Thinking back, I still regret not pummeling him. If Sam were real, he and I would've taken ol' Bart out.

Carson had been sitting in his usual spot by the dugout that day, thumbing through his notebooks and bag of stickers. That's when Bart got off the bench and wandered over. "Hey, big Berger brother. You know you're wearing your shirt inside out? Do you do that so it matches your brain?"

I may not be a fan of some of Carson's behaviors, but no one talks to my brother that way. I was about to tell Bart this when he turned to me. "Berger, what's wrong with your brother anyway?"

Sounding a lot more confident than I felt, I told him, "Absolutely nothing. My brother has autism, Bart. He was born with it. How about your brother? What's his excuse?"

Laughter spilled out behind me. Apparently, the baseball guys liked that one because Bart's brother is a seventeen-year-old pothead who has no time for Bart. It was a cheap shot and I know it. Bart can't help that he has a deadbeat brother. For a second I wished I could take the words back, but then again, how many times had Bart said mean things to Carson?

When we got home that day I laid it out for Dad. "We've got to do something about the way some kids treat Carson. He's a sitting duck for teasing with his stickers and flapping and trillion Superman shirts. Don't you see the way people look and whisper when they see us coming? They're mean. That isn't right!"

Dad just shrugged like it was no big deal. "It's fine. You'll always have kids who are looking to say mean things. But Carson doesn't seem to mind what others say, so don't let it bother you."

I wanted to yell, "No, it's not fine! And it bothers me because I don't want Carson being harassed!" But Dad got a call from Hazard Technical College, where he is Security Director, and had to run off to find out who set a fire in a dorm trashcan.

The other thing is, I care about making friends as much as I care about defending my brother. I worry about whether I can do either. Doing both seems impossible.

CHAPTER 4

Rourke and I get to be in the same school again.
~Carson

After tripping down memory lane to last summer's baseball game, I bring my head back to math class.

I sit at a table with Justin Christianson, a pitcher on my team. Bart's across the aisle. I do my best to ignore him.

"What field is football practice going to be on?" asks Justin. His voice is deeper lately and cracks on the word "practice."

"Field two," Bart replies as he combs his fingers through his dark hair. "Hey, Berger, you better be at football."

I give him a thumbs up.

"Good. And sit with the guys and me at lunch."

I nearly choke on my own saliva. "Sure!" I say, a little too enthusiastically.

Bart wasn't exactly *inviting* me but rather *telling* me to eat with him. Typical Bart manners. He's all but ignored me and treated my brother like dirt for years, and now he wants me to eat lunch with him? I should have told him, "When pigs fly!" But this is middle school, the land of cliques and popularity. It would be awesome to start the year hanging with the popular crowd, and following Bart might be my ticket in, even if I can't stand the guy.

Mr. Piper starts taking attendance. "Rourke Berger?"

"Here."

As he continues through the class list I wonder who the girl in front of me is. I can't see her face, but her hair is this deep chocolate color and so soft-looking I can't help but touch it. I pull my hand back and glance around, hoping no one noticed.

"Grace Elliott?"

"Here."

So that's her name. Grace Elliott. The girl with the chocolate hair.

After he finishes calling out names, Mr. Piper goes right into a forty-five-minute lecture on the importance of math in our world.

By lunch I'm famished and search the caf for Phinney. I forgot to ask what lunch block he eats. It's probably just as well if it's a different one, as Phinney doesn't think much of Bart and his posse. Of course, it's mutual. Bart, the self-proclaimed king of the in-crowd, thinks Phinney is a nerd. He's right, but Phinney's cool with Carson, which makes him an extra special nerd in my book and a true friend.

WHILE I'M STANDING in the cafeteria line inhaling the smell of spaghetti, my stomach tightens. When does Carson eat? Who will sit with him? Will this gnawing need to protect him ever go away? I'm starving, but putting food into a knotted stomach isn't fun. Inside my head, Sam insists that Carson is in good hands and I have nothing to worry about.

Bart is ahead of me waiting for the caf computer lady to come back so we can give her our lunch numbers. His loud voice makes me temporarily forget my twisting gut. "In social studies, I asked Ol' Pick n' Flick when it was going to be snack time, and he told me 'grade school is over, young man'."

"You mean he didn't flick you one of those fleas he pulls out of his beard?" laughs Justin.

"If he had, I would have eaten it because I'm starving!"

This gets a chuckle from all of us, even though I have no idea who Ol' Pick n' Flick is. When Bart makes a joke, everyone laughs no matter what. And I admit, it's great to laugh.

I move my lunch tray along to where homemade cookies and chocolate pudding catch my eye. I think of Mom's attempts at baking and how her cookies are always flat and somewhat burnt.

There are at least half a dozen signs stating "ONLY ONE DESSERT PLEASE!" Bart grabs two, but one of the dessert-ladies catches him. "Leave some for the rest of the students!"

Bart puts one back but grabs it again when she turns away. *Didn't his mother teach him any manners?*

We head toward a table. Supermodel Monica and her girl-group are seated nearby, giggling and looking five years older than the boys. It must be the makeup.

I'm the last to reach Bart's table and stand there like a dufus holding my tray. There's not a chair for me.

"Hi, Rourke!" calls Monica. "There's an extra place with us."

The supermodel is inviting me to sit by her? Heat moves up my neck.

"Everyone scooch down," Monica calls to her friends and pulls the chair out for me. What's with the red carpet treatment? First a Bart invitation and now one from Monica.

Bart shrugs. "Go for it."

Apparently I need his permission.

I take Monica's offer and start shoveling my spaghetti in. My hand shakes as I raise it to my mouth. It's good I'm sitting beside Monica and not across from her so I don't have to be distracted by her blue eyes. The girls chat on as though I'm not there, which is a relief. I have little experience talking to girls other than my sisters, especially when I'm wrangling slippery pasta.

As I dive into my chocolate pudding, I hear a familiar voice. "Rourke, I want to sit by you."

Carson has pulled a chair from somewhere, and before I can even reply through my pudding-filled mouth, he tries to jam it between Monica and me.

In his effort to position the chair, Carson loses his grip on his tray, and I witness the end of what had started to look like a promising middle school career.

<h1 style="text-align:center">CHAPTER 5</h1>

*I'm burned out from being a school social worker; teaching
science will be a relaxing change.*
~Miss Thompson

Carson's tray tips in slow motion onto Monica's head. She
gasps and bolts up from her seat as the spaghetti sauce
hits. Her shriek explodes across the cafeteria. "*Ahhhhh!* What
are you doing? *Ahhhhh!*" She flaps better than Carson.

Red sauce drips down her face as she sputters and wipes the
guck from her eyes. She is steaming!

Was it not a second ago that things had been going so well?
My ears throb and a dull roar whooshes through my brain.

Sam's face materializes before me. He looks disappointed
that I haven't taken action, so I jump up, grab my napkin, and
begin mopping Monica down, but she backs away gasping.

"What are you doing?"

There's a huge blob of chocolate pudding on her once-white
shorts, and it crosses my mind that maybe Our Lady of
Perpetual Light School is still taking late registrations. I could at
least apply.

Monica's girl-gang screams, and the guys howl as Bart points
at Carson, yelling, "Freak!" Every eye in the cafeteria is on us as
an eerie kind of silence surrounds me.

I stumble back and steady myself against a trashcan. My gut
clenches. First the near-hit by the bus, and now Carson coats

the next supermodel with spaghetti. But Bart's name-calling makes my blood boil.

I wobble forward, grab the neck of Bart's shirt into a tight wad, and yank him toward me. Angry eyes meet mine. "Shut up, Bart!" I mutter through clenched teeth.

"Everything okay here?" asks the lunchroom monitor.

Bart gives me a sleazy smirk and I drop his shirt.

Bart nods. "Sure is."

I turn to Carson. His face and Superman shirt have red sauce dripping from them but, oddly, it doesn't faze him.

Monica shrieks me back to attention. "Who are you?" She directs her ear-splitting question at Carson.

"Nice to meet you." He extends his hand to her. "M-m-my name is Carson."

"I don't care if you're the president! Look what you've done to my clothes!"

"Rourke is my b-brother. My best friend. I want to sit by him."

I find my voice and step in. "It's not his fault, Monica. Please don't yell at him. He can't help it. I'm sorry. It was an accident."

It's all I can offer.

Monica spins away from Carson and glares at me. I swear I see flames rolling from her nostrils. I back up even further, taking the trashcan with me. She looks like a bull ready to charge. The raging animal shakes her head, and the spaghetti flies. More shrieking. This time, it's from her friends who are getting sprayed.

Sam is yelling in my brain that it's Carson I should help, not Monica. Of course! Man, I can be so dumb. I should get that tray picked up. I turn, but some girl is already cleaning up the mess. Thank goodness, a Girl Scout among us.

Carson stands watching her, oblivious to the snickering and

insults. Girl Scout picks up Carson's fork and napkin and uses them to scoop the spaghetti from the floor onto his tray. She directs Carson back to the cafeteria line for a new tray of food. Good, someone's taken control while I stand like a frozen fool.

When Girl Scout returns with a rag to wipe up the remaining mess, I recognize her. My jaw drops. It's the girl from math with the incredible chocolate hair! I would probably still be staring, stupefied, if not for Monica's exit screech.

"My new outfit is ruined!"

The supermodel spins and stomps out the door wearing her spaghetti-and-pudding ensemble and is followed by two members of her entourage. I concentrate on gaining control over my breathing. I turn and see Carson has a new tray and is now sitting with my crazy neighbor, Peter Salzmann. I'm not hungry anymore. Girl Scout has disappeared. I wish I could.

As I dump my lunch tray I see Monica leaving the building with her adult twin. Her mother, I'm guessing. And they're laughing! Girls are weird. Shrieking and spewing fire one minute, laughing the next.

Luckily, social studies with Mr. Dunphey gives me time to air out my mind after the spaghetti storm. He instructs the class to spend the hour examining our textbook table of contents. Then I head to the gym for Phys. Ed. with Mr. Presell and sit on the bleachers while he lists his rules.

"If you chew gum, you write yourself an invitation to visit the principal." I watch his chest moving in and out with each breath. I hope he doesn't have a heart attack. He takes a huge drink from his water bottle, sucks in a breath, and moves on to the next rule.

Now I know why his nickname is Puddles. His shirt isn't

just damp under the armpits. It's soaked from his pits to his belt. I'm short of breath just listening to him huff and puff his way through this.

I allow my gaze to roam the rows in front of me. Phinney, Justin, and Girl Scout. I should thank her for cleaning up Carson's mess, but I'd rather forget about that lunch disaster. And Bart's here too. I can't believe I told him to shut up.

Five minutes into Puddles' rules, the gym door opens. I stiffen. Carson and another student walk to the bleachers with a teacher's assistant and sit down. I don't know whether to be glad —*I can keep an eye on him and help him*—or afraid what Bart might do to him. A pulsing sensation circles my right eye. I don't remember anything else Puddles says.

FINALLY! The grand finale of the day! I walk into life science and there she is, Miss Thompson, with her smile smoothing out the wrinkles in my world. She covers her class expectations, and with each word, my body melts into the seat.

Her face damp with perspiration, Miss Thompson sweeps her eyes across the class. "There will be science homework every day and if anyone is having trouble with it, I recommend you stay after school for help. I'll be in the room for forty-five minutes after the bell rings to tutor."

I anticipate needing a lot of tutoring.

<h1 style="text-align:center">CHAPTER 6</h1>

I don't know what people want. They keep changing their mind.
~Carson

The next morning at breakfast my sisters are still talking about their first day of second grade, while I'm feeding the dogs my toast under the table.

"Rourke," says Dad as he grabs his car keys. "Carson and the girls told us all about their first day of school last night at dinner. I guess we forgot to ask about your first day of middle school."

"Yeah, pretty crazy. I have lots of friends in—"

"I bet!" Dad interrupts. "I remember those first days—a little like drinking from a fire hose. Too much, too fast."

Dad kisses Mom on the cheek and heads for the door.

"Something like that," I mumble.

"Speaking of fast," Mom chimes in, "you'll have to be quick and walk Carson home every day before football practice."

"Mom, I'm gonna need help in science, so I'll be staying for after-school tutoring."

"Tutoring?"

"Yeah, science isn't easy for me. I want a decent grade." It isn't exactly a lie. What I didn't say is, "Miss Thompson helps me relax, and I don't want to wrestle with getting Carson home in one piece every day and end up late for football practice."

"Good for you, Rourke!" Mom smiles. "I'll figure out a way to pick Carson up. I look forward to seeing that A in science!"

As I set off with Carson and Phinney, I give Carson firm orders. "You HAVE to walk with us all the way to the front door of the school today."

Mr. Independent isn't having it. He flaps and whines, so I tell him, "Here's the deal. I'll let you walk the last two blocks alone again, and I'll buy you new stickers, if you stay on the sidewalk and don't run in front of the buses."

"Superman stickers?"

I can't help but laugh. He has folders full of Superman stickers. And Spiderman and every other superhero that's ever hit the big screen.

"Of course!"

"Hundreds?" Carson asks.

"As many as I can find."

Sam pats me on the back.

Phinney and I watch Carson walk to the school's main entrance.

"Do you know where I can buy a truckload of Superman stickers, Phin-man?"

He gives me a fist bump. "Online, maybe?"

In ENGLISH, Nicotine Nancy (aka Mrs. Harris) tells us we'll be reading *To Kill a Mockingbird*. As she strolls by my desk, I catch a waft of stale cigarette smoke from her clothes and practically gag. Maybe there's a sequel called *To Kill a Student* starring Mrs. Harris.

"But first," Mrs. Harris says, "we'll read *The Outsiders* by S.E. Hinton."

I look at the book cover. It looks old. Rudy asks the teacher a worthwhile question. "Why do we have to read stuff that's older than our parents?"

Nicotine Nancy leans over and breathes into Rudy's face. "Because it's classic literature, Ralphy." Rudy's face reddens. He's either mad she called him Ralphy or ready to keel over from her tobacco breath.

Our first assignment is an author study. I do a search on S.E. Hinton and find out the S stands for Susan. Why do authors use their initials instead of their name? J.K. Rowling, E.B. White. Maybe when I turn in my next paper I'll sign it RJ. Berger. Somehow it sounds more like a rapper than an author.

I read that the author was fifteen when she started writing *The Outsiders* and eighteen when she got published. My interest barometer goes up a few notches.

I forget sometimes that I like reading. There's so much other fun stuff to do, like sports and video games. But once I start reading, nothing else exists, not even my worries over Carson or girls or weird neighbors. Writing is the same way. It brings me to another world.

Mrs. Harris introduces the characters and assigns a chapter a night starting the second week of school. With characters named Ponyboy and Sodapop in the story, I'm skeptical about how awesome it will be. But this is school, and you read what you're told.

On the way to lunch Bart barks out an order. "Sit at my table today, Berger. I'll protect you from the next food storm."

My gut twists at the sound of his voice.

Bart motions to Carson sitting with his T.A. "I see they have your crazy brother back in his cage."

I clench my fists and glare at him, wishing the heavens would drop an elephant on him every time he says something nasty. Better yet, I wish I had the nerve to stand up to him. Telling him to shut up obviously didn't phase him.

I sense Sam urging me to make a decision: Tell Bart to stuff it or find somewhere else to sit. I like the second idea, but where do I go? The guys I want to hang out with are sitting with Bart. And Monica isn't about to invite me back to her table. Ugh! Middle school friendships are impossible!

I turn to the girls' table, and Monica catches my eye. She stands up and carries her tray full of beans and mini corndogs toward me.

I hold my breath.

"Hi, Rourke! Do you think today's lunch entrée matches my new clothes?"

She leans over and rests her tray squarely on my head. Bart and the other guys are still as statues, eyes bulging in anticipation of the great payback.

The blood is pounding so hard in my ears I barely hear her whisper. "I think your brother is cute." Then she twirls to show me every side of her perfect self before she giggles and sits down to eat.

I breathe out. Oxygen returns to my brain. The guys howl.

I have to hand it to her for being a good sport. Maybe she'd like to play tennis with me sometime. I barely get this thought completed when Bart makes an announcement.

"Monica's going to the movie with me Friday night." Makes sense: most popular boy dates most popular girl.

CHAPTER 7

Other people like hugs. Not me. I feel smothered.
~Carson

The second week of school, I start reading *The Outsiders* before bed.

"Rourke! I've called you three times. Did you set your alarm last night?"

"Huh?" I roll over and squint against the sunlight filtering in under my shade. The clock says 7:22 but my body is telling me it's still the middle of the night. I sit up slowly.

"Your hair looks funny," giggles Eva from the perch she's taken in my chair.

Sisters! I narrow my eyes at her and point at my door. Eva sighs and leaves.

I lean over and grab my *Outsiders* book from the floor. It's open to the ninth chapter. I don't know what time I fell asleep. I wanted to keep reading.

Ten minutes later, I'm dressed. Mom tosses me a muffin and shoos me out the door. "After I pick out new carpet and furniture for the living room, I'm taking you for a haircut after school today."

"No can-do, Mom. Football practice."

All day I think about that book. Are there kids like that? Without parents? Living by themselves, poor, and ending up in street gangs? In English class I look around the room. What if I knew a kid who had to fight just to survive, someone from the wrong side of the tracks fighting with kids like me who have parents and food and normal stuff? Well, normal except for Carson.

I think about the poem in chapter five, the one Ponyboy says to Johnny.

> *Nature's first green is gold,*
> *Her hardest hue to hold.*
> *Her early leaf's a flower;*
> *But only so an hour.*
> *Then leaf subsides to leaf.*
> *So Eden sank to grief,*
> *So dawn goes down to day.*
> *Nothing gold can stay.*

Nothing gold can stay. It's like a haunted spirit whispering to me.

Whomp! I jolt awake. Nicotine Nancy dropped a dictionary on my desk.

"Mr. Berger. You may sleep in my class, but snoring is where I draw the line." The whole class gets a good laugh.

"Remember, your assignment tonight is to read chapter two. We'll discuss it tomorrow."

CHAPTER 8

I never even knew Carson was different until I was eight.
~Rourke

It's LINK day! My feet can't stop wiggling. I've waited for this day forever!

LINK day is what our little town is known for—when every seventh grader in Hazard, Indiana gets assigned a ninth-grade buddy called a LINK. Since Carson has trouble getting the hang of sports, Phinney isn't into them (other than running), and Dad is always too busy to do guy stuff, it will be fantastic to be matched with that great someone who loves to throw the football around, shoot driveway hoops, and maybe go on to make sports history together!

Everyone in Social Studies has their eye on the door waiting for the ninth-graders to come. Mr. Dunphey insists we should take advantage of the fifteen minutes of class time before they're expected to arrive. "Let's review the definition of communities and the resources that best support them."

This gets a few moans.

Mr. Dunphey strokes his long thin beard, adjusts his wire rim glasses, and then picks something out of his beard and rubs it against his black corduroy pants. Whatever it is, it isn't coming off his fingers, so he flicks it, and it lands squarely in the wastebasket. Now I understand why Bart calls him Pick n' Flick.

Phinney gives me his *Did you just see that?* look. He holds up two fingers, and I choke back laughter. Social studies just got less boring with a basketball sideshow.

Finally the ninth graders arrive with their history teacher, Mr. Sawyer. When Carson walks in with them, my shoulders tense. His class is LINKed with mine? With the exception of P.E., my classes have become sacred ground where I do my best to follow Sam's advice and not obsess about my brother. And now here he is!

Carson's eyes sparkle when he spots me, and I can't help but notice how much he looks like me. Same body build, blue eyes, and wavy blond hair. But different shirts—all three of his are Superman ones.

"Are these energy-saving light bulbs?" he asks as he points to the ceiling. I shrug and motion him back to where his class is standing.

Worry clenches my middle. Who would get Carson for a LINK? I hope it's someone kind and they enjoy hearing about keys and stickers and light bulbs.

One by one the ninth graders announce their seventh-grade LINK. Phinney gives me a thumbs up when Carter Fields says his name. Perfect LINK match for those two! Both are science wizards and funny in a nerdy kind of way.

We're down to the last two ninth graders—Carson and that pimply arrogant Annabelle girl—and it's obvious my dream LINK isn't going to happen. It's a bummer for Emily Rubio too. She'll be stuck with the pimply one. Getting my brother as my LINK buddy would be a gift in comparison.

It's Carson's turn to make his announcement. I look up and give him a wave as he steals a rare look at me. He fumbles with a crumpled up piece of paper, finally opens it, and squeezes his eyes shut.

Just say my name, Carson.

He stares at the ceiling. I'd bet my new bat he's counting the ceiling tiles.

He looks confused and glances at me again. Eye contact isn't usually his thing. I nod to reassure him.

"Carson, introduce yourself," Mr. Sawyer coaxes.

Carson stares at the ceiling as though in a trance. After several awkward moments, his flat voice barks, "M-m-my name is Carson. My seventh-grade L-L-LINK is..."

Are those tears in his eyes? I've never seen him get anywhere near crying. Mom always says he doesn't really know how to show emotions.

Carson whispers. "M-m-m-my LINK is Emily."

"No!" I eject from my chair.

Boys are never linked with girls! It's a LINK rule.

Carson's announcement is like a spark on dry grass. Sometimes he gets things wrong. Maybe it's the autism talking, or nerves. But he knows me—his own brother! Why would he say Emily?

"Carson, it's me," I plead. "*I'm* your LINK."

"No, Carson's right," Mr. Sawyer says. "His seventh-grade LINK is Emily."

Which means my LINK is...

No Way!

CHAPTER 9

Something shakes loose inside me. Through a sea of confusion and snickers, the remaining ninth grader standing at the front of the room zeroes in on me through her thick glasses. Her snobbish, nasal-sounding announcement makes me want to peel her words right off me.

"I am Annabelle Doreen Jackson, and *my* LINK is you, Rourke Berger."

"Unbelievable," my voice squeaks. How can I make sports history with her?

I slide down fast and far in my chair, causing my head to smack hard on the back of it.

I hear screaming and shake off my brain fog just in time to get a look at Carson. *No, no, NO!* He has Mr. Dunphey's meter stick. His "just-for-teacher" meter stick.

"I want Rourke as my LINK!" Carson demands as he mounts the desk and begins to bash a piñata tied to the ceiling panels. Mr. Dunphey's eyes widen in shock. We had just papier-mâchéd the piñatas for a Spanish culture project. Someone grabs the stick from Carson, but it's too late. As candy rains down, I squeeze my eyes shut. This is not the way I pictured this day.

My temples pulse, and things grow eerily quiet. Everyone

freezes, including Carson, who is back on the floor. Mr. Sawyer moves toward Carson and corners him between the wall and a desk.

"Don't do that!" I shout at the teacher.

Carson's eyes search for a way to escape. Back and forth, up and down. When he looks up a second time, his eyes get hung up on a flickering fluorescent light. He grabs a chair, mounts the desk again, and beats the flickering monster to oblivion until the teachers manage to pull him to the floor, where he collapses into a seizure.

CHAPTER 10

The principal, Mr. Aspen, and the nurse show up. Once Carson comes around, they walk us to the nurse's office.

"I called your mother," says the nurse. "She's on her way."

Mr. Aspen shakes his head back and forth as he walks in front of us. Are Carson and I in trouble for ruining LINK day? At least I'm not being sent back to Annabelle.

The only light on in the nurse's office is a lamp. For some, this might have a calming effect. But I notice Carson focusing on it, and it's all I can do to breathe. I close my eyes. When I open them, Carson is pulling at his eyebrows and occasionally stopping to flap his hands.

Just this morning, Eva asked Mom why Carson flaps.

Mom told her, "It's Carson's way of calming himself when he's excited or stressed."

When Mom arrives, Mr. Aspen greets her as though she's just arrived at a party. "Thanks for coming, Ms. Berger!"

Mom rushes to kneel in front of Carson and brushes his hair off his forehead. "Carson, honey, are you okay? You had another seizure? I was hoping you were over those."

She looks beyond me to the principal. I feel invisible.

"Boys," Mr. Aspen says, "I think we need to hear what happened today."

Carson is shut down like a dead cell phone, so it's up to me.

I wait for advice from Sam. He tells me, *Take your time. Be kind. He's your brother.*

"Carson stole something from me today." My words spill out and flood the room.

Sam pokes me hard.

Everyone stares at me like I'm speaking a foreign language.

"I d-d-did not steal," whimpers Carson.

I roll out my defense. "We're told the purpose of LINK is to give us a good middle-school role model. We all wrote these great essays explaining our interests and our teacher promised a good match. The rules say that girls get matched with girls and boys get matched with boys. I got a girl, and not just any girl! I got that nasally, pimple-faced..." I draw in a deep breath. "I got Annabelle Doreen Jackson! Who in here thinks that's a good match?"

When Carson buries his face in Mom's lap I realize I'm shouting, so I tone it down. "Sorry, Carson. You're right. You didn't steal anything. None of this is your fault." I turn and look at the adults. "So whose fault is it?"

Mr. Aspen dips his chin and finds something interesting on the floor to look at.

"Everyone in this town talks this program up. Parents, teachers, kids—they tell us stories of how some LINKs become life-long friends. The Indianapolis TV guys were even here last year. Today was the day I was going to be matched with someone who gets me, somebody so awesome that Wikipedia would have to add a new definition for it!" My jaw is tight, and I barely recognize my own voice. I realize I'm standing. I place a hand on my twisted stomach and sit back down. "Today is supposed to be the best day for seventh graders. For me, it's the worst."

I have a whole lot more to say, like I'm tired of having to

make excuses to my friends as to why my brother acts the way he does, even though I know he can't help it. That I know I'm being selfish, but I just want a brother I don't have to worry about for ten seconds, to know what it's like.

Something is in my eyes, making it hard to see.

My throat is tight but there are more things I need to say. "Don't school people know anything about kids like Carson?" I hear my words break into pieces. "That cornering him is NOT a good idea? That maybe his class shouldn't have been matched with mine because he's so possessive of me that he always wants to sit with me, be my LINK, do everything with me, because—"

I run out of steam.

"Because Rourke's my best friend," Carson whispers.

I reach out to him and whisper back. "I know, Carson. You're my best friend too."

I look at Mom and fight the flood. "Did you know Carson goes postal when he stares at lights?"

Her red, wet face shakes back and forth.

CHAPTER 11

This isn't a good time for a family crisis. My boss expects more time from me.
~Mrs. Berger

On the way out of HMS, I notice Phinney on the steps. We've been friends since second grade when he ate his science experiment in front of the whole class. Swallowing a goldfish was the gutsiest thing I'd ever seen, and I couldn't stop laughing. That's the best thing about Phinney. He makes me laugh, and heaven knows I need to laugh. But today I'm not in the mood for his jokes or famous "don't sweat it" pep talks so I just slap him on the shoulder and keep walking.

I move as fast as I can to the backseat of our rusty van, where I squeeze between Hank and Beulah. They wag their tails and have no clue what just went down inside the school. I lean against Hank. Some of the nutty stuff drains out.

Carson hits his head on the car roof as usual, getting in the front seat. I know what he's going to say.

"I'm too b-b-big in this car." Yep, that's what he always says. "We should get a Jaguar. I like Jaguars. Rourke, do you like Jaguars?"

I ignore him.

"Rourke, do you like Jaguars?"

He asks me three more times. "Yes, Carson. I like Jaguars."

My sisters, the redheaded duo, are in the middle row.

"What took you so long?" whines Lucy. She and Eva had been waiting in the school office.

"Wars take a long time, Lucy," I mumble.

On the ride home, I stare at the back of Carson's head and think back to second grade when Mr. Fahey, our mailman, told me, "I see you've got a brother who needs special attention. Make sure you take good care of him."

It took me a couple years to know what he meant. Having Carson as a brother means nothing is ever normal in our house. I'm used to that, but after today, it won't be normal at school either. I close my eyes and picture Mom driving us far away to a land where no one minds if Carson is different and worry hasn't been invented yet.

When we arrive home, Mom flies into her multitasking mode. She reaches for all the empty gum wrappers in the car console, picks up her purse, puts her water bottle in it, settles her sunglasses back in their case, notices one bow of her glasses is loose, sets the glasses down, pulls out a notepad and scratches a note, rips the note off and holds it between her teeth.

I watch all this from the backseat, curious if my sisters are going to move sometime this century so I can get out.

"Rourke, please bring in the mail, and when you come back through the garage, honey, will you sweep it out? The dogs must have got into the garbage. It's a mess," Mom tells me. "But first, when you put your backpack in the house, hang it up on the high peg, not the short one, or Beulah will get into it again.

"And don't sweep out the garage in your new jeans. Run up and change before you do anything. And you might as well make your bed while you're up there, because for some reason you forgot this morning. And remember to feed Hank and Beulah."

I smile at the dogs. Dad brought the two red-haired puppies home the day my sisters turned one. I guess he thought Carson and I needed a present, too. Dad's a good egg. I just wish he was around more.

Our dogs used to be named Rex and Roland until Dad read me the *Hank the Cowdog* books. We laughed ourselves silly over Hank's life and his love for a beautiful collie named Beulah. After reading those books, I insisted we change our dogs' names to Hank and Beulah.

Mom turns and looks at me still seated in the backseat. "Rourke, are you all right? You don't look so good."

"I'm fine." I don't sound fine. I don't feel fine.

"Fine," she answers. She watches me for a few seconds. "Well then, what are you waiting for?"

For a genie to appear, and for Carson to be cured.

I drag myself out of the car.

"Mom, can Eva and I go to the park?" asks Lucy, twisting her red curls around her finger.

"Sure," Mom replies. "Have fun girls. I'll have dinner ready in an hour."

Just like that, they skip off without one single chore. Oh, to be seven again!

Mom turns to Carson, who is rocking back and forth in the front seat. "Carson dear, it's time to pick up the DVDs. They don't belong in our new living room."

Carson flaps. He doesn't like her idea.

"And no watching *Happy Feet* until the DVDs are put away."

More flapping.

Mom only gives Carson one thing to do at a time. He didn't inherit Mom's multitasking gene. I don't think any male has that gene.

Mom goes in the house and dials Grandma on the wall phone. Yes, we still have one of those. Actually, three: one on every floor. We must be holding out to get in the Guinness Book as the last family on the planet to own wall phones. I made the mistake once of asking, "Could we PLEASE get a cordless phone?"

Dad said he liked the wall version and went on to enlighten me with the history of the telephone. "The party line was the first version of Facebook. If your grandparents wanted to learn the latest gossip they just picked up the phone and listened in on the neighbors' conversations."

Groovy, Dad.

While dialing, Mom notices a bill from the dentist office. She spits out the note about fixing her glasses and hangs up the wall phone. I smile, imagining Grandma's face as she's left wondering who just hung up on her.

"Rourke, when was your last teeth-cleaning?"

"July."

July of last year was closer to the truth, but I hate that fluoride junk. So does Carson. He threw up from it. Ever since then, taking him to the dentist requires military intervention. And, it takes the Special Forces *and* the Navy Seals when he has his annual blood draw.

"I'm going to call to make a doctor's appointment for Carson," Mom says. While she dials, I pick up her cell phone and take it to my room. In theory, I share the phone with her. I tried convincing her I should have my own.

"Mom, I know second graders with their own cell phones."

"I'm not their mother," was her reply.

I call Phinney—but he doesn't answer.

CHAPTER 12

Counting things is one of my favorite hobbies.
~Carson

Dad arrives home three hours early from work. His expression screams, *Heavens no, your mother didn't call me and tell me my boys' actions in school today means we should get out of Dodge.*

"Hey, Rourke!" Dad gives me a high five. He hasn't done that in months. Next he ruffles Carson's hair. "Carson buddy, how are you doing?"

"I'm putting my DVDs away."

Carson never detours. One task at a time. When he's done with the DVDs, Carson heads to his room.

"Skipping *Happy Feet* today?" I ask. No response.

After I finish my Cinderella chores, I walk into Carson's room.

His favorite song is playing: "Red Solo Cup." The green army soldiers he and I used to play with are lined up around the room. They start on his desk, continue across the floor, and up onto the windowsill. Others march under his bed and, where the little green guys come out the other side, Carson duct-taped a cardboard arch to the carpet. The soldiers parade under it and behind the door. A small Superman figure leads the entire brigade. And he has a rule: no one messes with his army.

I can't tell if Carson knows I'm here. He didn't look up when I came in. I remember when Mom told me that kids on the spectrum don't have good eye contact. And the counselor at the sibling camp I went to with Carson said ASD affects behavior, even simple social stuff like saying, "Hey, Rourke!"

I watch Carson write the number 172. He turns the page. 173. He's always counting something. The number of cracks in a parking lot, the number of times the church bells ring—even the number of age spots on Grandma's arms. The school psychologist says this is how he processes information.

174.

Carson has his sunglasses on. He wears them in the house but never outside. Sitting cross-legged on the floor, he cradles a light bulb he took from his lamp.

"What?" Carson finally notices me. The curls fall down his forehead and make him look younger than fourteen. 175.

"Nothin'. I just came to see how you're doing."

"Fine."

At the sound of his small, soft voice, my insides loosen. I kneel beside him. "Did you want to be my LINK, Carson?" Maybe I shouldn't go there.

Silence. 176. Without looking up from his important numbering work, he asks, "Who-who–?"

He stutters when he isn't concentrating on his talking. Or when he is stressed, or for no reason at all.

"Who-who would you pick, Rourke?"

"Carson—" My throat catches and I have to concentrate on not crying.

177.

"Carson, if they lined up the ninth-graders on the fifty-yard line of the football field, and I could only pick one to be my LINK buddy, do you know who I'd pick?"

"Me." There's no emotion in his answer. It's just there, like a shirt that's been ironed flat. 178.

For once I'm glad he doesn't look at me. He'd take one look at my leaky eyes and ask me if I got hurt.

"Yeah, you," I whisper.

Downstairs I hear Mom and Dad talking so I turn off "Red Solo Cup," which makes Carson flap. Dad has on his oldies station again. "Hey Jude" drifts up through the floor vent. Carson hums along, rocks back and forth, and makes up his own words to it. Hearing him makes me hurt inside. He is just doing his Carson thing, but mean people make fun of him over things like this. I wish I could rip the autism part of him right out and blow it to bits so no one could hurt him again.

"Hey Jude" ends and the radio gets turned off. Mom and Dad are in a serious discussion about Carson's meltdown at school.

"So you think the flickering light in the classroom caused Carson to have another seizure?" Dad asks.

"I'm not sure. But we should ask Dr. Graham about it. Migraines and things like seizures can be triggered by flickering lights."

"But lights haven't been the cause of his other seizures. And he hasn't had one for over a year. Angie, I thought his seizures were behind us."

"Me too." Mom's voice is a sad whisper.

I look at Carson to see if he's taking any of this in. 205.

"Something happened when Carson stared at those lights today, Jason. It must have been awful for Rourke to see."

A heavy sob from Mom floats up—and I'm done listening to the heat vent news. I reach over and press "start" on Carson's CD player. "Red Solo Cup" returns and Carson sings along to it. For some reason this makes me smile. Carson likes a country song that talks about drinking beer from a red plastic cup. 212.

I leave Carson to his papers and numbers and walk to my own room.

Lying on my bed, I stare at my Indianapolis Colts poster on the ceiling.

More seizures. It's not enough that Carson has autism? Now he's having seizures again? It isn't fair.

The lump in my back pocket reminds me I have the cell phone, so I call Phinney. "Know any decent schools I could transfer to?"

"The Lady of the Holy Pants and Perpetual Light School is across town." I can always depend on Phinney to make me laugh.

"Hmmm... I hear the tuition is high. That would set my parents back a bit to send me there."

Phinney suggests a bit of advice. "Maybe returning to deal with a broken piñata won't be as bad as the high expectations at Lady of the Holy Pants."

Mom calls us to dinner, but I just pick at my food. Mom isn't the best cook, and I'm used to that, but tonight it's worse than usual because it's seasoned with the disappointment of LINK day.

Lucy whines about the spaghetti. "What are these things?" She holds up a chunk.

"Garbanzo beans," Mom tells her.

"Gross. Why can't we go to a fast food place to eat?" asks Lucy.

Dad makes a funny face at her. "Well, Lucy, when I was your age we didn't even have fast food."

"Oh, here we go!" laughs Mom. "Your Dad and one of his stories of life in the olden days."

"Why didn't you have fast food?" asks Eva.

"Because all the food was slow."

Lucy laughs so hard spaghetti squirts out of her nose. Any other night this may have been funny to me. But I'm still in a bit of a shock over the day's events and worry about what tomorrow will look like.

<h1 style="text-align:center">CHAPTER 13</h1>

I wish I had a best friend.
~Bart

Things happen in schools. You know, when you don't hand in your math assignment and sirens go off because it alerts your teacher to send you to the homework police.

But certain things are only whispered about, like folklore. Things that, if they happen at all, should happen in the deep, dark woods where only fairies live and magic potions repair the damage—not in front of your seventh-grade friends.

But if your brother is Carson Berger, there are no far-off places. Because his problems aren't quiet. My friends are going to see them or at least hear about them. There's no disguising the fact that he'll always need someone to live with him and drive him places and make his meals and keep him from getting run over by a bus and...

Okay, Sam. You're right. I've got to stop dwelling on this. Or at least try.

Maybe Carson was upset he couldn't be my LINK, or maybe his eyeballs stuck on that bright something and it triggered an electrical explosion in his brain. Either way, it's not good. I'm petrified something horrible is happening to him.

CHAPTER 14

Rourke needs to chill.
~Phinney

Girls have an odd perspective. After LINK Day, the girls in Mr. Dunphey's class act like I'm some kind of a hero—which I certainly am not. Maybe they just feel sorry for me that I'm stuck with Allergy Annabelle. The only time I spend with her is when we have game time on Fridays.

The first Friday we meet to play chess, Annabelle asks, "What's wrong with your brother?" This seems inappropriate.

"He's friends with Superman."

Annabelle glares at me and blows her nose. "I'm not stupid you know." I'm not sure what that means, but I find myself feeling sorry for her and let her win. Maybe she gets teased and bullied too. She could probably use a brother to defend her. And maybe an imaginary friend like Sam too.

I look across the room at Carson and Emily playing Yahtzee. He loves being her LINK. She has patience with a capital P. If only Carson hadn't looked at the light on LINK day, it would have saved a lot of frustration and maybe even the piñata. I wonder to this day where all the candy went. Maybe in Mr. Dunphey's desk. Or his beard.

AFTER TUESDAY'S FOOTBALL PRACTICE, Phinney runs to our house, his jet-black hair sailing behind him. I consider myself a decent athlete and can run fast, but no one catches the great Phinneas McGee.

We sit on my front steps and stuff ourselves from a bag of chips he brought over.

Out of the blue Phinney asks, "What would you rather have your brother be like? Bart the Great or Carson the Great?"

I laugh to hear him refer to Carson as "the Great."

"What? Those are not even choices. Carson is...well, Carson. And Bart only *thinks* he's the greatest."

"Oh, so you're picky, huh?"

"I just want Carson the Normal, Phinney. Is that too much to ask?"

He punches me in the arm and says his famous line. "It takes all kinds of kinds."

CHAPTER 15

The best part of my day is seeing my keys all lined up.
~Carson

Puddles (aka Mr. Presell) needs to enroll in a physical education program of his own. When you're round and old, you can pull a muscle getting a drink of water. So I can't say I blame Puddles for choosing P.E. activities that aren't so strenuous. Like archery.

I'm not sure I'll like it, because I'm a team sports kind of guy. The only archery I've done is on my Wii, but this is the real thing. I mean, who has a real bow and arrow anyway?

Puddles tells us we need a shooting partner and has us count off by twelves, which sounds kind of dumb but, whatever.

There are thirty kids in our gym class. We get to the third round of counting off by twelves and stop at six because we run out of people. I'm a seven.

"All right people." He pauses to take a breath. "Find the other students with the same number as you and go stand by them." He sounds as enthusiastic about this as if he's telling us to watch plastic break down. "Most of you will only have two at a target but some targets will have three."

I was paying attention when everyone counted. The other seven is Grace Elliott, the Girl Scout. This nervous butterfly thing flaps around in my gut. I look out of the corner of my eye in her direction. Geesh! She's looking at me! She must have been paying attention to the count too.

"You better learn to love this person because they'll be your partner for the next three weeks, and don't even think of asking me for a change. I don't care if they smell. You're stuck with 'em."

Mr. Presell moves so now Grace is in my direct line of vision. She doesn't look friendly, and I bet she stinks at archery. I hope I don't have to help her hold her bow or something weird like that. If I have to pair up with a girl, why can't it be someone friendly like Maggie or Abby?

"Now, if your partner fails to follow my rules and fires an arrow into your behind, let me know ASAP and I'll make a reservation for them in detention." We all chuckle, and Puddles gives us a fake smile. His face is red and dripping wet. He pauses a while to catch his breath and then tells us how to shoot and score.

"The most important part is my whistle commands, and you know I love to blow my whistle. Let me demonstrate."

- "One blast, shoot."
- "Two blasts, get bows."
- "Three blasts, pick up arrows."
- "One long blast, *stop shooting!*"

Puddles gives his lungs a break. "We'll have a written quiz on whistle commands Friday. I better see a perfect score or you're looking at fifty push-ups."

I glance at Grace. She doesn't look strong enough to last through ten push-ups, let alone fifty.

Puddles emphasizes his golden rule. "Remember, people. Once you are done shooting, *do not retrieve your arrows*. Wait! W-A-I-T."

He's panting now. "Never, and I repeat, never go and pick up your arrows until I give the all-clear blast of three whistles. Why do I care? I don't, but my kids need to eat and in order to feed them, I need a paycheck. If I get sued by your parents because you have an extra hole in your body, I won't have a job, and my kids will starve to death."

We get the picture. Go get some oxygen, Mr. Presell.

I glance at Carson. He's gonna have trouble waiting for that whistle. Thank goodness for the T.A.

Yes, Sam. I know—stop worrying about Carson. I wish I could convince my stomach not to worry.

We spend a long time practicing Mr. Presell's "Eleven Steps to Archery Success." Our shooting stance and how to nock an arrow onto the string, draw it back to the side of our face and anchor a finger at the corner of the mouth, plus a few more I've already forgotten.

I didn't know fingers could sweat, but mine do. The bow is stiff and foreign in my arms. But everyone's in the same boat. I'm too preoccupied with my own bow to notice whether Grace or Carson are getting this.

"People. It's now time to put what we've learned into action."

Puddles blasts his whistle two times which means one person in each group can pick up a bow from the rack and walk to the shooting line.

Maybe I should be a gentleman and let Grace go first, but she motions me ahead.

Fine.

When I hear the one-blast whistle, I take an arrow out of my quiver and glance toward Grace. *Ugh!* She's watching me.

I place the bow on my toes the way we were taught. I remember my open foot stance position, nock the arrow, and hook the bowstring into the groove. Step by step I go through the shooting procedures. I center my grip and raise my bow arm, drawing it to eye level. My arms shake. I bet Grace's eyes are on me.

Other kids have already let arrows sail. There are whoops and laughter for targets hit or missed. I aim for the bullseye and begin moving my shoulder and elbow back. Man, it's tight! I release and the arrow flies, barely catching the top of the target before slipping to the ground.

Oh well. First try.

Many of my shots don't even hit the target. I have two arrows left. The first one drops to the ground by my shoe so I try again and manage to get it to sail toward the target. It nicks the outside edge and hangs on to produce a score.

This is kind of embarrassing.

Bart laughs. "Hey Berger, you're shooting as bad as your brother over here. Remind me not to rely on you for food when we're called up for the Hunger Games!"

My last arrow manages to hit the outside blue ring for five points.

Okay, so I'm not Robin Hood.

Grace is up, and I'm relieved to stand back and watch her make a fool of herself too. I smile and give her my good-luck-you'll-need-it shrug. No smile from her, but at least she isn't begging for help. I mean, this isn't the Olympics.

I check out how Carson is doing. It looks like the T.A. has things under control. He's on seizure medication now, so that's one less thing to worry about.

I turn back as Grace pulls out her first arrow, and for some weird reason, I notice her fingernails. They aren't painted like a lot of the girls' nails, certainly not like Monica Monahan's. Hers are always some shade of shocking pink and have little gemstone sparkly things glued to them. Grace's are chipped and her fingers and right hand are scratched and stained.

Grace pulls her first arrow up and out of the quiver onto the bow. That's when I notice it—a nasty two-inch scar on her left wrist.

Not bothering to check her stance or take her time with each step as Mr. Presell insisted, Girl Scout eyes the target. I know she's going to blow this. In one motion she sets, draws, aims, and shoots. Right into the bullseye.

My eyes nearly leave my head. Mr. Presell's booming voice bellows, "BULLSEYE on target seven," which causes a momentary ceasefire while kids look to see who nailed the first one. Cheers erupt.

"Beginner's luck," I mutter. Grace gives me a dirty look.

I bet she took this class before at her old school.

"Berger! Maybe you better take her with you to the Hunger Games for protection!"

My face burns.

Grace picks up her next arrow. I study her face and the way she draws the string to the side of her cheek. Smooth, flawless motion. BINGO! Another bullseye.

No way.

"Hey! You're awesome!" says Abby Johnson, girl jock destined to be a pro something someday. Name a sport. She excels in it.

Everyone stops shooting even though there's been no long whistle command. All eyes are on Grace, and they follow her third arrow right to the center of the target.

Whistles and applause flow through my stunned brain.

"Never mind, Berger. I'm taking her to the Hunger Games myself! That will leave you with plenty of time to take care of your brother."

It's Big Mouth again.

Puddles honks the whistle three times, giving us the okay to retrieve our arrows.

Grace puts her bow down with a stone-face. Any other kid would be doing cartwheels after shooting like that! I don't know why, but I want to find out more about this Grace Elliott—and that nasty scar on her wrist.

Sam is in my ear urging me to say something.

"Good shooting!"

She lowers her head and stiffly smiles. "Thanks."

Alert the media. She speaks. And smiles! Well, kind of.

CHAPTER 16

Tonight is "Back to School Night" at my sisters' school.

"Just make sure you stay in the same room with Carson all the time so he doesn't escape." Dad gives me last minute instructions before heading out the door. It's like I'm taking orders on how to keep a mountain lion in his cage so the neighborhood isn't terrorized.

"You don't have to feed or entertain him, just keep him safe for an hour or so. Sound fine?"

"Fine."

For the most part it's easy "babysitting" Carson as long as he stays in the house. For a couple years there, we had to have the police on speed dial as he'd slip out when Grandma babysat us.

Tonight Carson is watching the Hazard City Council meeting on cable so I wander up to my room with Dad's laptop to check out archery tips on the internet.

"Rourke Jason Berger! Come down here right now!" Mom's welcome-home greeting blasts up the stairs.

They're already home? I fly down the steps.

"Holy buckets!" screams Lucy.

We all stare at the same thing. Carson is sprawled out next to his bike in the living room. Or shall I say, his bike parts. The greasy chain is on exhibit on Mom's new white sofa.

Mom's gonna shoot him. And me.

"What's up, Carson?" Dad's voice has a hint of amusement.

"The dogs are helping me fix my bike."

Hank licks a bike tire and Beulah rolls her eyes up at me as she contentedly chews on a greasy glove.

"Mmm... I see that." Dad squats down beside him and observes Carson's greasy hands work at getting his kickstand undone from the bike frame.

"I can help you fix your bike, Carson," Eva says. I smile inside. I love that girl.

As steam rolls out of Mom's ears, Carson picks up Dad's toolbox and dumps it onto the new carpet.

Mom gasps and marches to the sofa, working her way around the fish hooks and nails and random other junk scattered about. Her face is pinched as though she just caught a whiff of something rotten. She slowly picks up the black chain with two fingers. It leaves a perfect figure-eight grease mark. I hold my breath, waiting for the explosion.

"Did you know he was doing this?" Her voice is low and controlled as she eyes me for a sensible answer.

What can I say? That I sat and watched Carson ruin her remodeled living room?

"Mom, it's fine." I figure it's worth a shot to try her "fine" quote.

One look tells me she doesn't think so, and she fumes off to the kitchen, returning with a bunch of cleaning products and brushes. I reach for them, but she yanks them away and sprays something strong on the sofa. It drips black streaks down the side onto the carpet.

I may as well kiss my allowance goodbye, until I'm thirty or so.

Dad and I help Carson move his bike parts and tools back to the garage. Since Dad isn't handy with mechanical stuff, he loads the bike parts into his trunk. "I'll have the bike repair shop fix 'er up like new for you, Carson." He gives Carson a pat and chuckles.

"I'm sorry, Dad. I was supposed to watch him."

"Water under the bridge, Rourke."

Through our heating vent intercom system I hear Dad tell Mom that maybe a white sofa wasn't the smartest choice for our family.

Mom grunts. "I thought the same thing about that old motorcycle you bought that still doesn't run."

That Rourke Berger is so out of it lately. He must be lovesick.
~Mr. Piper

I can't see her wrists from where I sit in math.

Ever since archery began, I find myself thinking about Grace a lot. A person isn't born an archery expert. So where would a seventh-grade girl learn to shoot like that?

And is she doing something to her wrists? That's a nasty scar. I've heard about people cutting themselves. Maybe she's a worry wart like me.

"Rourke Berger! Are you there?" It's Mr. Piper.

I jump and everyone laughs.

"Rourke, I've called on you three times, and I don't think the answer is on the back of Grace's head that you've been staring at the last ten minutes." More laughter fills the room as heat crawls up my neck.

He repeats the question about the difference between a ray and diameter of a circle, and I get it right. Math is easy—when my mind is on it.

THE WHISTLE-COMMAND QUIZ in archery is a breeze. Carson didn't have to take it. Everyone else, except Rudy Daley, gets a hundred percent. I bet he got some of the questions wrong on purpose. He's a kid who does what he can to get attention.

As we all stand in a circle watching Rudy do his push-ups, Bart yells, "Better lay off those triple bypass burgers, Rudy!"

I cringe for Rudy's sake. And then Carson does something strange, even stranger than his usual strange stuff. He gets on the ground and does push-ups beside Rudy. No one says a word as we watch this unusual pairing. I bite my lip and watch their bodies rise and fall through a blurry fog.

When they're done Rudy's red face is streaming with sweat. He slaps Carson on the back. "Thank you, buddy."

I glance at Bart who rolls his eyes at me. What's with him?

IN THE SECOND week of archery Grace and I aren't exactly talking up a storm, but I compliment her on her rounds, and once she said "nice try" when I hit the second ring from the bullseye. When I whiff a shot, she giggles. For some reason her laughter makes me all warm inside. Up until now she acted like there was some grand prize on the line.

Then she's absent four days in a row, which is strange. I mean, it's the last week of archery with a quiz tomorrow. Where is she? Did she move again? Wait a minute. When did I start worrying about a girl more than Carson?

Sam tells me that maybe I was just born to worry.

GRACE RETURNS but offers no excuse for her absence. She looks a mess. Her bright eyes don't look bright, and her usual smooth hair is a tangled nest. Even I can tell it needs brushing.

She has bruises on one of her arms, and she only hits the bullseye once for the skills test.

"Have you been sick?"

Grace tenses and looks at me with dark, guarded eyes.

What? I'm just trying to be nice and ask a simple question. You know, for conversation.

Her face turns cloudy and she turns away.

"You okay?"

No response. She grips the bow tight and bites her lip.

Maybe I'll change the subject.

"I thought maybe I'd improve my shooting game while you were gone. Ya know, when you're not here staring me down." I make sure I say this like I'm kidding. "But as you can tell, I'm still a lousy shot."

"You need practice."

Whoa. A whole sentence.

She steps in front of me. As she leans in close and meets my eyes, her breath is on my face. "And I'm not staring you down."

Oh.

Her eyes soften as she turns away but not before my ears grow hot. What's with all this blushing stuff? I don't remember this happening in sixth grade. I look away in time to hear Bart scream as Carson's arrow sails into his leg.

"I wanted to take the archery test," I hear Carson's explanation to Dad through the heating vent. "So I shot the arrow. I-I-I didn't mean to hurt anyone."

"Carson," Dad says, "your arrow barely nicked Bart's jeans. Plus, they're rubber tipped anyway. No worries. It's fine."

It's my turn to roll my eyes. No worries? It's fine? I want to kick something.

CHAPTER 18

Rourke needs help.
~Miss Thompson

At the end of September, Nicotine Nancy plans a quiz on *The Outsiders,* so the Phin-man and I get together to study at his house.

"Phinney, do you think there are kids in Hazard with problems like Ponyboy and Sodapop?"

"Oh sure. I saw a couple gangsters in Central Park last night."

"No, I'm serious!"

"Since when do you get all whipped up about stuff in a book?"

"I don't know. I mean, the stuff Carson and my sisters do drives me crazy. But, no parents? Man, what would I do if something happened to them?"

"I bet Mad Marlys would take you in!"

"Oh, now there's a cheery thought. I'd rather live under a bridge."

Later, in my own room, I stare at my worn copy of *The Outsiders* and think maybe life is pretty good right now. No recent Carson disaster other than shooting Bart with his arrow. Football, Sam, Phinney—all good. Grace—??

I open to chapter nine. Tears sting my eyes as I read Johnny's words to Ponyboy, "Stay gold." The last line of Robert

Frost's poem eats at me. *Nothing gold can stay.* Is that how life works? Things are good. Until they aren't.

I copy the poem onto a piece of notebook paper and pin it to my bulletin board. The effort exhausts me.

ONLY A FEW WEEKS into school and Bart and Monica are an item, which figures. Monica is way out of my league anyway, and I doubt she wants to date someone who has a brother that gave her a spaghetti bath. Plus, my grades aren't exactly honor roll status, so I can't let distractions like Model Monica pull me off course. I need decent grades to stay in football.

Miss Thompson's after-school tutoring not only helps my science grade but my spirits. I only stay for ten minutes as football practice is right after school, and Coach Cole doesn't tolerate tardiness. Miss Thompson is so nice and (did I mention?) pretty.

"Rourke, I believe you understand science, but sometimes in class you look like you're in a different world. You just need to be more confident and focus. What do you think?"

I shrug. I can't tell her tutoring is part of my escape plan from everything I worry about.

"Rourke."

I don't know why, but every time she says my name, a layer of me gets peeled away.

"How is it to be in the same school with your brother this year?"

"It's...fine." My chest tightens. I've sunk to using my parents' favorite line. If I were honest I'd say, "My nerves are frayed, my stomach is a mess...and it's not just because of Carson."

"It can be hard to have a sibling who has extra challenges."

I ball my hands into fists on my lap as the heat moves up my neck and face, threatening my eyes. I hop up. "I gotta go."

As I grab my backpack, she smiles, "It can't be easy."

Her words light a flame to the gas can. I turn toward her and fire off, "I'm not looking for easy! I just want to know I'm not going crazy!"

I instantly regret this. I'm shouting at Miss Thompson? What's wrong with me?

"He's back, isn't he?"

The world tips. I reach out to the chair to steady myself.

She knows the answer so I don't bother replying. Maybe I don't need help in science anymore. No matter how nice it is to spend time with Miss Thompson, I don't want to talk about my make-believe friend with her again.

CHAPTER 19

Who is Sam? I hear Rourke talking to him sometimes.
~Carson

The moonlight splashes against my bedroom wall. My alarm clock reads 2:31 a.m. I've been in and out of restless sleep for hours.

I try to think about regular stuff. Carson's got his bike back in one piece. Mom got her sofa and carpet cleaned. Dad's motorcycle is sitting on the curb with a "for sale" sign on it. I guess my allowance didn't quite cover the cleaning bill.

But then not-so-regular stuff drifts into my head. Sam and I have a conversation about the day. And Miss Thompson's voice keeps popping into my head. *"He's back, isn't he?"* How does she always know what's going on with me?

It all started in fourth grade. I was delivering a book to Miss Thompson for my teacher. She wasn't in her office so I sat and looked around at the posters and quotes about kindness on her wall and thought about the troublemakers she dealt with as a social worker. While I waited, I started talking aloud to my make-believe friend. Sam had been "with me" since the day Eva asked the simple question, the day my worry knot formed.

As I chatted away to Sam, I noticed Miss Thompson in the doorway. I don't know how long she'd been standing there, but long enough.

For the rest of fourth grade, I spent thirty minutes every

Monday telling Miss Thompson about my pretend friend and how he helped me take care of Carson.

"Why do you call him Sam?" Miss Thompson had asked.

"It's short for Superman and Me. Because Carson always wears Superman shirts, and he's my brother, and I like to imagine he has superpowers the rest of us don't know about."

I remember her saying things like, "Many people have imaginary friends. Someday you won't need Sam and he'll go away."

Miss Thompson was right. A year later, when Carson was in middle school, Sam just kind of disappeared, and I was fine with it. But now he's back, along with a growing worry about any little thing that happens.

CHAPTER 20

I wish I had a brother.
~Phinney

Sunday night, Phinney comes over for pizza. We head to the basement for some gaming. Carson is on the floor organizing his stickers.

"Hey, Carson, buddy!" Phinney calls.

Without looking up from his stickers, Carson mutters, "Rourke says you dress like a turd."

"WHAT!" Phinney and I respond in unison.

"Carson, I said nerd, not turd." Carson acts like he didn't hear me, and Phinney just laughs.

"How is your after school date?" Phinney asks as we settle onto the sofa.

"Huh?"

"Is she willing to wait for you?" Phinney concentrates on the basketball video game we're playing.

When I figure out Phinney is talking about Miss Thompson I throw a pillow at him. Hard. He unleashes his crazy laugh, and I end up laughing, too.

The next morning I feel like "something the cat dragged in," to quote my father. More nightmares. The worst one was about creepy green-eyed aliens taking over the world after they ate too many desserts. I tried hitting them with my bow but kept missing.

I want to stay home and sleep, but I hate to miss classes. I have to keep my grades up. Mad Marlys doesn't care what you do in study hall, so I try catching up on sleep there.

I get a midterm warning in English and social studies because I didn't turn in some assignments. The day after the pink slips are mailed, I race home from school three days in a row to check the mail. When they finally come, I rip them to shreds so my parents won't see them, then tear back to school for football practice. Middle school is a lot of work.

CHAPTER 21

There's always a calm before the storm.
~Mr. Berger

"Carson seems to be behaving himself so far this year." Dad scoops another spoon of cereal into his mouth while reading his motorcycle magazine.

It's almost the middle of October, and my stomach is in its usual morning knot. Mom insists breakfast is the most important meal, so I pick at my bagel.

"As you say, Dad, there's always a calm before the storm."

Dad has all these sayings like "if the shoe fits" or something is on "its last leg." But his favorite is the storm one, which freaks Carson out. Last summer when Dad used that line, Carson holed himself up in the basement bathtub for hours because he thought we were all going to get blown away. When he came out Lucy told him it was raining cats and dogs which sent Carson right back to his tub sanctuary.

I hope there isn't a storm brewing with Carson. I haven't thought about having to transfer schools since LINK day.

"Football going okay?"

I smile. "Fantastic!" It's not often Dad inquires about my sports.

"Does your hair fit into your helmet?" Eva giggles her question at me.

"Why can't girls play football?" whines Lucy.

"Because twerps like you would drive the coach crazy!" I swat her head as I get up to leave.

"It's a dumb sport," says Eva. "You get hurt."

"Football isn't dumb. It's the best part of middle school so far! Hey, Dad! Coach tells me I have great hands." I fantasize about making a winning touchdown catch and having Dad witness it.

"Great! Then use those great hands and take out the garbage."

So much for trying to get Dad all excited about my athletic skills.

"You're coming to my scrimmage today, right?"

"Sorry, Rourke, the college is flying in some big-wig politician to speak, so my security crew and I will be working late."

If Dad would ever look at me, he'd see right now how disappointed I am.

Football practices have been boiling hot, but it's satisfying to sweat after sitting in school all day. We've had two games with teams from neighboring towns, but today we are scrimmaging the eighth graders. This is always a great rivalry, and families come to watch. Except my dad, I guess.

The eighth graders expect to win and have been trash talking us all week. We want to cream them, but of course it's never been done.

As I warm up with my team, I see my whole family, including the dogs and Dad! I gallop to meet them.

"Dad, you came!"

"Yep! Here I am! I have to see how your great catching hands work!"

"Rourke, I'm here too," says Carson. "I want to see if your hands work too."

Laughing, I give him a slap on the back, which makes him shake.

"My hands are working great, Carson!"

Hank and Beulah lick my shoes until Lucy and Eva pull them away for a romp around the school grounds. Someone stops to give Hank a bite of a hot dog.

"Hmm... I hope that hotdog doesn't reappear on my carpet later," Mom says.

I run back onto the field and see Carson alone on the bleachers. Sam tells me he'll sit with Carson, but I know Sam isn't real. I force myself to look away and stay focused or Coach won't play me.

I notice the eighth graders warming up on the south end of the field. They're bigger than us, but we have some fast guys. Maybe we can outrun them, if we could ever hold onto the ball.

"This team has a bad case of fumble-itis," Coach yelled at practice one day. "The cure is practice, practice, practice!"

Carson is still sitting alone. My gut tightens. Isn't there one person in this school who will be his friend?

We win the toss and choose to receive. The eighth-grade kicker, Rusty Edwards, sends the ball sailing end-over-end down the field. Anthony Laine attempts to catch it but fumbles. He apparently hasn't been practicing enough. He manages to pick it up and scrambles to the thirty-five-yard line.

Bart is our quarterback, of course. I start in as receiver, but seventh-grade football isn't much of a passing game. The first three plays are on the ground and don't get us the ten yards we need for a first down, so we punt the ball away.

On their third down, the eighth graders score with the quarterback running it in from thirty yards. If I had been in as safety, I would have mowed him down. There are no goal posts on the practice field where we play so they go for two points and miss. The score is 6-0.

On our next possession, running-back Calvin Jaspers fumbles during a hand-off from Bart, and the eighth graders have the ball back. I guess Calvin needs practice, too. They take advantage of our mistake and score again on a twenty-two-yard touchdown pass. Another short pass into the end zone gives them two extra points and we are down 14-zippo.

We have eight-minute quarters with a few water breaks scattered throughout. On our next set of downs, Monica and her girl group start cheering, but to no avail, as the game stands at 14-0 at halftime.

Coach Cole sends me in as safety at the beginning of the second half. The safety position helps defend the pass play. The other team doesn't seem to be passing much either, but then they did get one score on a pass. Things are kind of back and forth the third quarter until a speedy eighth grader returns the ball sixty yards. I take him down ten yards from the end zone.

The fourth quarter is pretty boring unless you count all the substitutions. Coach Cole follows through on his promise to get every player in the game. I am back in as a receiver with Justin.

With ten seconds left and the score still 14-0, we get the ball back. I line up right. The play will be a fake hand-off, and then Bart will look for an open receiver, probably his favorite, Justin.

I glance to the sideline to establish my location on the field. The field has a wall of tall pine trees on the west side blocking the afternoon sun. Between two of the trees, in broad daylight, there's a boy with his back to the field, and he's peeing!

I gasp. Carson! I don't know why I'm shocked.

Bart is calling signals. "Fifteen!"

I move my eyes desperately back and forth from the spectators to Carson. *Has anyone else noticed this? Is everyone blind today? I sure hope so.*

"Twenty-two!"

Still peeing! I can see the stream arcing toward the trees. He must have had a gallon of soda.

"Five!"

I panic when I see a bunch of younger boys running toward Carson, pointing and howling like a pack of wolves.

"Nineteen!"

The snap from center.

I scream at the top of my lungs. "Carson! Get behind the trees!"

Carson can't help but hear me. It's a mistake to have yelled at him though. He turns around and zips up his fly for the whole county to witness.

Calm is done. The storm has arrived.

The thundering sound of running football players jolts me back to the game. I propel myself forward from the line and turn toward Bart. I don't see the ball, but I figure out where it is when it makes solid contact with the top front of my helmet and throws my head back.

How in the world did it get to me that fast?

The football spins upward against a blue sky before gravity takes over. I spring up, snatch it, and land on both feet before sprinting into the end zone dragging a tackler with me. We get the two extra points, and the final score is 14-8. Respectable loss, all things considered.

I butt helmets with Bart and get mauled by teammates but train my eyes on the trees. Carson is nowhere in sight, but the laughing boys near the trees kill my joy over my touchdown. I'm praying those kids won't leak it to the whole school. No pun intended.

Sam's voice seeps through to my heart. *It's not the end of the world. Be cool.*

Before I turn off my light and get into bed, Dad pushes my door open and pops his head into my room. "Rourke, don't worry about Carson. We'll talk to him about appropriate places to pee. It'll be fine."

Not one word about my great catch.

CHAPTER 22

It would be nice if my family showed up for one of my games.
~Bart

Archery is over, thank goodness, and we've moved on to the annual fitness test. It consists of curl-ups, the sit and reach, push-ups, and the one-mile run. Since exercise is good for blowing off steam, I can't wait to start.

The mile run takes us by the football practice field. "Hey, Berger! After your brother peed on those trees I'm surprised they aren't dying off by now."

Ah man...if Bart knows about this, the entire town of Hazard knows.

On Friday, the fitness test scores are posted. I have the third best boys' score in seventh grade! Carson has the lowest, not because he isn't fast or strong, but because when you decide halfway through the mile that you're done and "don't feel like" doing push-ups, you end up with a low score.

Someone (pretty sure I know who) drew a freaky-face beside Carson's name. Sam calls this "childish behavior." I call it mean.

For the girls, Grace is number two behind Abby Johnson who beat some of the boys in push-ups and the mile.

After the grueling week, I guess Puddles thinks we deserve a break, so we fool around playing kickball and suck on freeze pops. Abby and Grace walk in front of Phinney and me as we head back into the school.

"Grace, you are speedy!" says Abby. "You should go out for cross country with me."

Phinney agrees. "Yeah. First you mop up in archery, and now you almost knock off our number-one running girl!"

Grace laughs. "Actually, I *am* in cross country."

"You are? I've never seen you at practice."

"I volunteer every day after school so I can't come to practice, but I run on my own."

This is the most I've heard her talk. Phinney and I stop at the door with Abby and Grace long enough for me to glance at her hands, but she's moved them behind her back.

Curious, I ask, "Where do you volunteer?"

Grace looks out of the corner of her eye at me. She acts like I'm grilling her every time I ask a simple question.

"At the homeless shelter."

"Hazard has a homeless shelter? I didn't even know we had homeless people."

Grace ignores me and turns the conversation back to running. "Coach Gina says I can run in the meets as long as I have someone sign off on my practices. In fact, I'm running in Monday's meet!"

"All right!" cries Abby, giving Grace a high five.

On Monday, Coach Cole lets us out of football fifteen minutes early due to the heat. I grab my backpack, slam my locker, and sprint across the highway to the golf course. I wanted to watch Grace run in the meet, but the school website showed the JV running at 3:45, so she'd be done by now.

The warm orange and yellow hues of autumn look like a painting and I can't help but whistle my way to the course. A pack of varsity girls are still running their race across the fairway. It takes me a minute to spot Phinney among the spectators.

"Hey Phin, how's it going?"

"Great! But it's a hot day to run. I hope it cools off for my meet tomorrow."

"Yeah, football practice was brutal today. How did Abby and Grace do?"

"Well, Abby pulled a hamstring warming up so she's not running, and Grace didn't run JV."

"She didn't show up?"

"Oh, she's here all right. Running varsity."

"No way! She qualified for the top seven?"

"I guess." Phinney checks his stopwatch. "The first runners should be coming up this hill in about…one minute."

A long trail of runners is stretched out along the north side of the golf course.

"Where is she?"

"Can't tell from here. The leaders are in that tight pack headed toward the turn that brings them up Heartbreak Hill. And the rest are still on the straightaway."

I strain my eyes against the bright sun to zero in on the top of the hill. The first runner's head bobs into sight, and the crowd gets loud.

A girl in a blue jersey with Decker High School printed across it leads. Close on her heels is Shontell Davis, the top runner for Hazard. I don't recognize the next four as they're from other schools, but these first six girls are in a tight race.

"Run! Dig in, Gina."

"Come on Shontell—get her."

"Get 'em Decker!"

"Run Hazard!"

The last hundred yards is tight, but it's clear the Decker girl has saved enough to take it home. Wait! Another Hazard jersey tops the hill.

"Well, look at this!" Phinney says and screams, "Go Grace!"

Wow. Star archery expert, star runner. There are surprises around every corner with this girl!

Once on the flat, Grace picks up speed, and she's smoking. Her body is erect, strong, and pumping for the finish line. With half the distance to go, she passes four runners, and the home crowd is screaming for her.

"Run Hazard! Go Hazard!"

No one knows her name except Phinney and me, and I'm too stunned to speak. "Kick it, Grace! Kick it!" Phinney has beat-boxed my eardrum.

She gains on Shontell, leans into the finish line, and finishes a hair in front of her. The Decker runner wins, but Grace is second. Unbelievable!

Coach Gina and Shontell run over and hug Grace. I can't believe it! I mean, new to town, running with the high school kids, and then taking a first team spot!

Phinney rushes to Grace and I follow. She's walking off her run when she notices us.

"Where did you get those legs, Grace Elliott?" Phinney asks.

Like someone turns on a faucet, Grace bursts into tears. Instead of looking like a winner, she looks broken. Before Phinney and I can figure out what to say, she turns away, and we let her go.

"What did I say wrong?"

"No clue."

CHAPTER 23

Who knew dancing with girls would be fun!
~Rourke

D ance is our new unit in Phys. Ed.

Mom is pumped. "Hey, this means you and I can practice dancing. Your dad has never liked it."

"Hey!" Dad tries defending himself. "I've never said that."

Mom gives him a friendly poke.

"Mom, I don't like it either. The only reason I do it is because Pudd—I mean Mr. Presell—is making us."

"What dances are you learning?"

"He has us doing the polka and the electric slide. And my personal favorite, the worm."

Dad laughs. "I can't picture Mr. Presell dancing."

"He's surprisingly coordinated."

"I can't believe the school is using my tax dollars to teach you to dance like a worm!"

Mom laughs as she multitasks her way through dinner prep. "Dear, when we were kids we learned disco in school. What's the difference?"

"The difference is we never admitted to our parents what kind of useless junk they were teaching us in school," insists Dad in an amused sort of way. "And I wasn't paying taxes back then!"

The next day we partner dance. We rotate so no one is stuck

with one person. My first partner, Maggie Martin, pretty much steers me around the gym floor and talks my ear off.

"How long have you and Phinney been friends?"

"Mmmm. A long time."

"Where does he live?"

"On Linden Street, by the water tower."

"What's his middle name?"

"What? I don't know."

"Can you ask him?"

"Maybe."

"Does he like any of the girls in our class?"

"Uh, maybe. We don't talk about girl stuff."

"Yes, you do."

What? Girls can read minds?

"Tell him I think he's cute."

Nerdman Phinney? Right-o.

Jennifer Bailey and I dance awful together. She goes one way and I go the other, looking like two short circuit robots bumping around.

I notice Carson dancing with his T.A. and counting the steps aloud. One-two-three, one-two-three... Sam and I smile as Carson moves surprisingly well. Who knew dancing was his thing? Maggie cuts in to dance with him and Carson beams.

Next, I dance with Abby. We laugh and exaggerate the steps to pretend we are on *Dancing with the Stars*.

When I rotate to Grace, I anticipate a long, cold silence.

"Hi, Rourke."

She said my name! Write it in the history book!

"Hey, Girl Scout."

No! I didn't just say that.

"What did you call me?" She squints at me with a hint of a smile tugging at her lips.

Puddles' command saves me from answering. "Grab your

partner and remember—for the waltz, it's one-two-three, one-two-three."

"I'll explain later." *What a moron I am.*

"One-two-three, one-two-three."

I'm pretty decent at the waltz. But Grace isn't.

"Whoops! Sorry. Sorry!"

Girl, it's just gym class!

When she trips, I grab her to steady her. She's so uptight, but I have to admit I enjoy her mistakes. Grace is a few inches shorter than me, so I get to watch her black lashes lie against her cheeks as she watches her feet.

"Man, I stink at dancing!" She stumbles again.

"Finally something I can do better than you!"

"A LOT better!" She looks up at me and giggles at herself. Her smile melts me. Several times we have to stop and restart. I review the steps with her so she knows what direction she should go.

Wait until Mom hears I taught a girl to dance!

We give up trying to get our steps right and make up our own moves until Grace steps on my untied shoelace and I fall.

"Wow, I need some serious help!" She giggles as she pulls me up.

"The Rourke Berger dance studio might be able to fit you in for some private lessons," I tease.

"Sure! And you can come to my private archery range, and I can show you a thing or two about shooting an arrow straight."

"It's a deal." And I hope she isn't kidding. "Where do you live?"

Her forehead wrinkles.

Mr. Presell stops the music to make an announcement.

"Before the bell rings I'm going to teach everyone one more dance called the Seventh Grade Special. It features Rourke and Grace's signature dance move."

I glance at Grace and she's giggling with the best shade of pink in her cheeks.

"This dance is where all the boys untie their shoelaces, and when I start the music, we'll see how long it takes the girls to step on the laces and make the boys fall—just kidding!"

Carson starts clapping and calls out, "I know this dance!" He leans over and unties his shoes then stares at his feet.

Rudy bends over and unties his shoes. All the other boys follow his lead.

Carson says, "St-st-start the music, Mr. Presell."

The music starts, and before long there's a lot of tripping and laughing.

CHAPTER 24

Our neighborhood used to be quiet, even boring, until the Salzmanns moved next door.

"Jason, these hillbilly neighbors are building an eight-foot fence!" Mom screeches through clenched teeth. "And those chainsaws aren't just hurting Carson's poor sensitive ears, they're driving me crazy!"

"Sounds like they're fixer-uppers." Dad laughs but Mom is steamed.

"But we moved to this cul-de-sac because it was quiet, no distractions or craziness to get Carson worked up. I mean, listen to this."

A window opens. I can't help but laugh. Maybe I get my worrying from my mother.

"Those chainsaws run non-stop. What are they building over there? An ark? And what's with that junky little camper on the street?"

"Angela, we have to get used to them. Remember how our neighbors had to get used to Carson when we first moved here?"

"Yes, but—"

"At first they weren't so happy with him opening their mailbox to check for free stickers in their junk mail. Now they realize he's harmless; they don't even notice when he stands in front of their house counting their windows."

Mom sighs. "All I can say is I'm glad we're going camping this weekend so we can get away from this noise for a couple days." She turns to me. "Rourke, are you and Carson still going to play baseball?"

"Uh-huh."

"Okay, you have about two hours. By then I'll have everything packed to go."

Mom has a point about the new neighbors and is right on about Carson's sensitive ears. Storms, doorbells, fireworks, my sisters' piano duets, even the furnace fans bother them. Too bad Gramps can't borrow one of Carson's ears. Gramps can barely hear the person next to him. But I'm pretty sure Carson can hear a raindrop fall in Ohio.

"Carson! Ready to do some catching?"

"Where's my glove?"

"Same place it always is."

"In the garage bin."

"Yep."

Together we head to the baseball field behind our house where five other boys are warming up. Peter Salzmann sits near his fence watching. He kind of gives me the creeps.

This field is the reason I love my neighborhood. It comes with its own baseball diamond! Whenever the neighbor kids get together to play, it's a blast. Carson can't get the hang of baseball rules, but ever since Sam suggested I make him the all-time catcher, he loves it. Carson misses more balls than he catches, but it's one of the few things we can share, so I'm sticking to my choice for catcher.

After the third inning Carson stands up. "I need a break."

As he stands, Kenny-the-Moose swings, and his bat

connects with Carson's forehead. Carson walks to me with blood gushing out of a nasty gouge near his hairline.

I don't like blood. My knees go weak, and something bitter fills my throat. When Sam orders me to help Carson, I fly into action and pull off my Hank Aaron shirt Aunt Kelly sent me for my birthday a couple years ago. In the distance I see Peter Salzmann stand up. I wrap the shirt around Carson's head and steer him home.

"Am I still the all-time c-c-catcher?"

"Maybe."

Mom is in the middle of packing food for our camping trip when we show up. "Rourke, where's your shirt? You—oh, no! Carson! What happened?"

Carson doesn't even peep. I wish he would scream or cry to let me know he feels something. He stares right into my eyes the whole way to the hospital while I hold the shirt tight on his head. I can count on one finger how many times he's done this. A lump forms in my throat as our eyes lock.

The ER is a lot more lenient than restaurants when it comes to letting you in without a shirt. They use the superglue stuff on Carson's head instead of stitches since he goes nuts with needles. As they hold the two sides of the cut together, my stomach flops, but I get to hold Carson's hand. He almost never lets me touch him, so it's beyond special to do this for him.

"We've been to the emergency room five times with Carson," Mom says as she sighs for the hundredth time. "Maybe baseball isn't for him. We should just let him organize his keys and stickers. It's safer."

"But he loves being catcher, Mom."

I look down at the bloody Hank Aaron shirt. I wish there was a way to let Hank know his shirt saved Carson from bleeding to death. I wish there was a shirt that could save him from autism.

I don't want to go camping anymore. I stare at Carson with wet cheeks and worry about what river he'd fall in or what cliff he'd slip down. Carson got so ripped off. What kind of a life is it with no friends and no way to keep safe? Other kids his age will soon have their driving permits. Dad said Carson would never get a license. Getting to drive a car is one of the best things to look forward to. Well, that and sports. But Carson stinks at sports, too.

WHEN WE GET HOME from the hospital, Dad is with my sisters. Even though they are identical, Carson and I have always been able to tell them apart. And their personalities are like night and day.

Lucy inspects Carson's forehead from about six inches away from his face and crinkles her nose. "Ya-ouch! Carson, that looks awful."

"Carson," Eva whispers as she peers up at him. "Wanna watch your favorite show with us? It'll make your head feel better."

"Yes. I w-w-want to watch the legislative session."

Yesterday, his "favorite" show was David Young playing Für Elise on a recorder on public television. Sometimes it's the local school board meetings. If he doesn't understand how baseball works I'm curious what he's getting out of these shows.

Sam reminds me Carson's mind works different, and I shouldn't compare him to others.

WE SPEND an hour loading the van and car-top carrier with camping stuff. I used to love camping, but last year Carson insisted on sleeping beside me on the inflatable mattress. He has to have four layers of blankets on. It helps him feel safe, Mom says. Well it makes me *hot*! I pushed them off, but somehow I found them back on me. By morning I felt like I'd spent the night in a sauna.

"It's part of the whole sensory thing," Dad told me. "Being wrapped in heavy things gives Carson's body feedback and makes him feel secure."

I know. He'd told me a million times. Was I being selfish to think, "What about me? Does anyone care what makes me feel secure?"

We are stuffed in the car amongst our camping gear, waiting for Carson.

"Run up and get him, Rourke," Dad says. "He was in your closet looking for something before I came down."

I fly out of the van. He better not be in my room!

He isn't. He isn't in any room or any closet or anywhere to be found. After a neighborhood hunt, Dad calls the police. A police dog goes into Carson's room and sniffs his clothes. His packed duffel bag stuffed with nothing but Superman shirts is on his bed. Beside it is the bandage from his head injury. The dog sniffs that too. The police take a description and photo of Carson and ask a lot of questions.

"What if he has a concussion and is blacked out somewhere?" Mom is a mess.

"Where will Carson sleep? He'll get cold." I've never seen Lucy so concerned.

Sam's trying to calm me but it's not working. I go to my room and sit on the edge of my bed, doubled over with stomach pains. I see Peter Salzmann pacing back and forth in the street. Did he do something to Carson?

For forty long hours volunteers comb the town, the woods,

and the fields. No one sleeps at our house. I tell the police my suspicions about Peter so they question him.

When I was younger, there was no worrying; we were just brothers playing in the sandbox, pulling the dogs' tails, and wrecking our mattresses. I used to help Carson line up his collections of superhero action figures and keys. But where is he now? What if we never find him? I spend the weekend thinking the worst. Between waves of nausea I listen to Sam reminding me to breathe.

Sunday morning at nine-thirty, the police chief knocks on our door.

Mom's face has no color as she anticipates his report.

"No sign of Carson anywhere."

He asks more questions, plus some he'd already asked. "Could he have stolen a car? Does he have a credit card? Does he know how to swim? Who are his friends? Is he dangerous? Suicidal?"

After the chief leaves, Dad's eyes are red and Mom can't stop walking in circles.

I run to the garage and sit on the firewood box. Tears sting my eyes as I kick at the bin of baseball equipment.

"Carson, where are you?" I squeak out a pathetic whisper. I pull his catcher's mitt out of the pile and put it on. I hold it to my nose like the police dog, hoping I can catch a scent of Carson, but all I smell is sweaty leather. I pound my right fist into the glove and then hold it open, staring into the emptiness of it.

A baseball falls into the glove. I blink, but it's still there. I hesitate before reaching out and touching it to check if it's real. Am I imagining baseballs too?

I jerk my head back and stare into the dark rafters. There he is, sitting, his legs dangling down.

"I-I-I won't come down unless I can be aw-aw-all-time catcher again."

"Carson! What in the world? *Mom! Dad!*"

CHAPTER 25

This is getting weird. I worry about other people's worries.
~Rourke

"So are you going to ask her out or what?"

I roll my eyes.

"Monica's taken, Phinney. I don't need Bart and his thugs beating me up."

"I wasn't talking about Monica." He stares at me with a grin. "You like her and you know it."

I give him my "who are you talking about?" look.

"You honestly don't know who I'm talking about? Well, here are two clues. She's the only pretty girl in seventh grade who got that way without an ounce of makeup, she stares at you every day as you leave math, and she can shoot an arrow with the accuracy of William Tell."

"That's three clues."

"Whatever. You know who I mean."

"I'm not asking her out. I'm not asking anybody out." I kick a rock back and forth with Phinney as we walk home. "Plus, she's too..." I hunt for the right word. "Gloomy."

"Well, you know what I say?"

"Yeah, I know. It takes all kinds of kinds."

"Uh-huh. Plus, the winter dance is coming up, and you could at least dance with her."

"She's a lousy dancer." I smile as I remember dance class.

"But you have your signature move you could do with her."

I punch Phinney's shoulder until he convinces me to stop. Phinney. Sometimes he drives me nuts with his advice. It's like I have three mothers: Phinney, Sam, and Mom.

"I doubt Grace thinks school dances are for her. But I know who wants to go with *you* to the dance," I tease Phinney.

"Miss Thompson?"

"Ha! Maggie Martin."

"What? How would you know that?"

"She thinks you're *cute*."

"Right. You're making this up."

"Why would I make it up? She told me when she was busy dancing on my feet in Puddles' class."

Phinney's face glows beet red, something I've never seen.

"So there's your date for the big dance, Phin-man! Don't say I never did anything for you. By the way, what's your middle name?"

"It's Gomer. Why?"

I laugh so hard I have to run to the bathroom and pee. Wait until I tell Maggie.

My social studies book is stuck. I wiggle it until it breaks free from the mess on the bottom of my locker.

"Is it later yet?" I turn, and there's Grace. I can't believe she walked up to me, talking.

"Huh?" I'm buying time.

"You told me you'd explain later."

I put on my best confused face even though I know exactly what she's asking.

"You called me 'Girl Scout.' What's that all about?" I can't tell if she's mad or just curious. Or flirting? Okay, probably not that.

I pretend I'm hunting for something in my locker, but she pushes it closed. That's when I see them—bruises on her wrists. Just visible for a split second before her long sleeves slip down and cover them.

Distracted by the bruises as well as her boldness, I tense and swing my backpack over my shoulder.

"It's no big deal." I shift my eyes away from hers, which are way too close and aren't going to stop staring a hole through me until she gets an answer.

Bart walks by and yells, "Practicing your signature move, Berger?"

Justin Christianson chimes in, "Hey, if it isn't the ol' Grace and Rourke dancing duo!"

My face grows warm. And Grace isn't leaving. Time to fess up.

"Okay. Back on the first day of school, when you helped my brother clean up his tray and the floor? Well, you were like a...a Girl Scout. Ya know, doing a good deed and...stuff." I sound stupid.

Somehow I manage to meet her eyes.

"Oh. Cool. And thanks for coming to my cross-country meet."

She turns to walk away, but I catch her arm. "Thank you for helping Carson when he dropped his lunch tray." My voice sounds thick.

Her eyes grow soft and watery as they meet mine. "It's what Girl Scouts do. We save people."

Her eyes linger too long. I'm pretty sure she isn't just referring to Carson.

CHAPTER 26

I have to be careful what I tell people.
~Grace

"Hey, Girl Scout!"

I know I'm pressing my luck.

Grace turns and waits for me with her hands on her hips. "I can't believe you just yelled that down the hallway for everyone to hear—Mr. Fred Astaire."

"Who?"

Her jaw drops. "You don't know the most famous dancer of all time?"

"I guess not, but thanks for the compliment. And I thought that title belonged to Michael Jackson. Or Mr. Presell."

Her eyes crinkle at the corners as she giggles. "Never mind!" She's different today. Perky.

Grace stops at her locker to ditch her math book. Before she closes it, I notice a stash of granola bars and juice boxes on the bottom. And a boatload of chip bags. The kind we have in the cafeteria. Why is she hoarding snacks? Is there an approaching famine I didn't get the memo about?

I don't want to ruin the moment so I ignore the food. We head to the cafeteria, collecting a few stares, mostly from girls.

We meet Phinney who eats lunch the block before ours. He steps in front of us, forcing us to stop. "I hope you two are ready for taco-licious Tuesday!" he dramatically announces and then moves on with a wink for me.

"Phinney a close friend of yours?"

I smile. Now she sounds like Maggie. "Sure is, the best money can buy. We're on a year-to-year contract, though, as BFFs, so I never know whether someone might steal him away."

Grace giggles.

"Hey, remember our agreement? How I would help you dance decent if you teach me to get an arrow in the red zone?"

As she reaches for her tray she laughs sarcastically and raises her eyebrows. "I didn't say you'd ever get good enough to hit a bullseye."

She's making fun of me. Or is it just teasing? Where am I supposed to learn this stuff about girls? "Well, I'm not sure a clumsy dancer should be allowed to own and operate an assault weapon."

She narrows her eyes and gives me an accusing look. "Very funny, Fred. Name the day and time, and I'll be at your house for my first dance lesson."

Seriously? "Is it okay if it's on the Wii and it's called 'Just Dance'?"

She throws her head back and laughs. "Lame! But count me in."

"How does this Saturday work?"

"Two o'clock?"

"Perfect!"

Did we just make a date? I see Sam nodding.

The dessert lady isn't on duty so I take two pieces of cake. I'm feeling lucky today.

We each go to our usual spots to eat—Grace with a couple of girls from math class and me with the guys.

I can't stop smiling, and my tacos never tasted better. Until I notice Peter Salzmann sitting by Carson. The worry knot is back.

CHAPTER 27

Rourke has the perfect family.
~Grace

G race is coming to my house! The butterflies in my gut are working overtime. I'm afraid she'll cancel, but I am more petrified she'll show up.

If she comes, I'll ask her about her bruises. How can I casually bring that up?

"What happened to your wrists?" Too direct.

"You look like you've been wearing handcuffs." Definitely not the way to go.

Sam thinks it's not a good idea to ask her today.

It's 2:05. She's late. I bet she'll call and tell me she had to volunteer at the homeless shelter. Part of me is relieved. Even though Grace seems more upbeat lately and talks to me, I wonder if it's short lived. Will she retreat to her secretive self? Like Robert Frost's poem, *Nothing gold can stay.*

I pace. Wait! She's here!

Grace told me she walks everywhere so I'm surprised when she steps off the transit bus. It's freezing out so I'm glad she has a ride. Maybe I should've asked my parents to pick her up. I'm new at all this.

I watch from my bedroom window. She walks with confidence to our front door. Her gaze takes in the neighborhood. She stops and stares at the Salzmanns' house.

Who wouldn't? Five barking dogs and a security fence makes the place look more like a prison yard than a home. She probably lives in one of those mini-palaces near the golf course.

Then she waves in the direction of their house. I stretch to see who in the world she's waving at. It's weird Peter. Sitting outside in a camping chair. It's winter! Who does that?

I run to let her in before she makes it to the doorbell. Sam congratulates me for saving Carson's eardrums.

Thankfully, Mom isn't home so she won't be grilling Grace. Mom's real estate work takes her out of the house a lot of weekend hours. Driving clients around and showing them property until they find their dream house takes a while.

"This is my dad. Dad, this is Grace."

I can tell Dad is holding back in the question department. He probably had a mom like mine so he knows what it's like to be in my shoes. In fact, when I think of Grandma Penny I'm positive he did. Every time Grandma comes over, she quizzes us on everything from history trivia to clean underwear.

Dad says, "Rourke tells us you are quite the archery pro."

Grace smiles. "Well, he's quite the dancer so we thought we could help each other out."

"He also says you're a star runner on the varsity cross-country team this year. You must come from a great running family."

"My mom and I...we..." Her voice catches and she looks away. "We used to run together. She's the reason I run."

"I bet she's proud of you."

Grace bites her lip and looks away.

I jump in to change the subject. "Ready for your first dance lesson?"

"Sure!"

As I follow Grace into our rec room, nervousness crawls over me. Dancing in gym class is one thing. But now I'm sweating and questioning why I thought a dance lesson was a good idea for a first date.

"I'll be right back."

I take the steps two at a time up two flights and grab my deodorant stick. More is better.

By the time I return, the Lucy and Eva Show has invaded. They're rocking with the dance video, and Grace is right there with them. I watch from the bottom of the stairs as my nerves take a break.

"Come on, Fred!" giggles Eva.

What? I'm gone for a minute and Grace has already shared her pet name for me?

Eva pulls me in to dance. The four of us twist and spin and make up silly dance moves with the dogs prancing around us. The twins love to dance and sing, and since Grace has hit it off with my sisters, I don't make Dad kick them out. Plus, they take the pressure off me.

Carson appears from nowhere with his sunglasses on and stares at Grace. I cringe a bit, but Grace doesn't seem to be bothered. When Carson grabs her hand and dances with us, I remember his moves in dance class and figure, why not? The smile on his face is worth a million bucks!

After an hour of dancing, we're hot and thirsty so I take Grace upstairs for something to drink. I grab the cookie jar and watch as Grace downs four or five. I guess she worked up an appetite. Maybe this is the right time to ask her about her bruises.

But Lucy and Eva come running in and grab cookies.

"You have such pretty hair," Eva strokes Grace's head.

Giggling, Lucy says, "She's not a dog, Eva! Hey Grace, do you want to hear our piano duet?" Without waiting for an answer they run to the den and pound out a few verses of Heart and Soul.

Carson has followed us like a shadow and has his eyes locked on Grace. I wish he still had his shades on so his staring wasn't so obvious. I don't understand why he has so much trouble with eye contact and yet he stares.

I nudge Carson and mumble, "Stop staring." The flapping begins. Oh boy, I shouldn't have said anything. I sneak a glance at Grace but she's looking at the cookies.

"Do you have stickers?" Carson asks Grace.

She nods. "A few."

"Can I have them?"

"Well, I don—"

"Dad!" I call out. "Carson needs you!" But Dad's gone to walk the dogs. Once again, the disappearing Dad act.

"Carson really likes stickers," Eva giggles as she returns to the kitchen.

"Cool," Grace says. "I'd like to see them sometime."

Carson dashes out of the room and up the steps.

"Helloooo! I'm home!" It's Mom. "It's wonderful to finally meet the girl who is such an archery whiz! Seems a bit of an unusual sport, especially for a girl."

Here we go with Mom's Interrogation 101.

Grace shrugs. "Not really. I just like to learn things I can put to use and not waste time on silly things."

A crease forms between Mom's eyebrows before she takes up her line of questioning again.

"I see. And where did you learn to shoot arrows?"

"Dad taught me."

"Is there an archery range somewhere in Hazard?"

"Uh, I don't really know."

"So where do you practice?"

"We just set up our own targets."

"You mean like tin cans?"

"Sort of." Grace's answers are getting shorter, and I'm wondering how to cut Mom off.

"Doesn't your mother think a bow and arrow is dangerous?"

Grace's eyes cloud over. She searches the floor for her answer.

I attempt to save her. "Mom, Mr. Presell taught us archery safety."

"We need to go to the store." Carson is back and budges in between us. He's carrying two huge jars of stickers. "I don't have many stickers left."

Lucy looks into Carson's face and says, "Carson, what are you talking about? You've got zillions."

"Yes, so don't get all bent out of shape," I add. "And please apologize to Grace for interrupting."

"I'm not bent. I'm a regular shaped boy."

Lucy and Eva giggle.

"How many zeroes does zillion have in it?" Carson continues. "I didn't know I had a zillion stickers."

Mom casts a line to get Carson off the sticker train. "Carson, has Rourke introduced you to Grace?"

Peering into one of his jars, Carson replies, "I-I-I already know her. She cleaned up the mess I dumped on that m-m-mean girl. I need more stickers."

The back door opens. "What did I miss?" Dad is back with Hank and Beulah who are noisily drinking from their water bowls.

"What mess are you talking about, Carson?" Mom needs details.

Naturally my parents turn to me for an explanation. I give them nothing, other than a disgusted headshake. This is what my dating life is going to look like: one big circus show with Mom as the ringleader and Carson and my sisters as the main attraction.

"It was a long time ago and no big deal," Grace says, trying to let it slide.

"Hank is s-s-staring at Grace. Why can't I?" Carson asks.

Eva giggles and pets Hank.

"And what's this about a mean girl?" Mom pushes.

I can't stand it anymore and, a little too loud, say, "Carson's talking about Monica, and Monica's pretty, Mom. Not mean." *Why did I just say that in front of Grace?*

"Monica is one of the hot chickens at the school," Carson adds.

I choke on my lemonade and start coughing.

"Hot chickens!" Dad calls it out like the hotdog vendor at a ballgame. Eva and Lucy practically fall off their chairs laughing.

Grace covers her mouth and giggles.

I'm still recovering from the lemonade in my windpipe while Carson gives the news, "I dropped my lunch tray the first day of school."

"And?" Mom is wasting her time being a realtor. She'd make a killer detective.

Carson enjoys his part in all this. "My spaghetti flew all over the hot chicken's hair." Carson laughs so hard he snorts. "And all over h-h-her clothes." This time we all laugh until we're laughed out. Mom has tears running down her cheeks, and I'm holding my belly, because my twisted stomach is laughing uncontrollably.

Why is something so awful when it happens but later it's so hilarious you laugh until your face hurts? Some of the Carson episodes affect me like that.

Once we recover, Mom tells Grace at least three times how nice it is she helped Carson when he dropped his tray.

"I should be heading home," Grace says.

I guess I won't learn about those bruises today.

"You can't stay for dinner?" Mom offers.

Grace eyes the counter where Mom has a pan of vegetarian lasagna prepped to bake, as well as a store-bought apple pie. Grace gives a regretful headshake. If she only knew about Mom's cooking, she wouldn't look like she's missing something.

"Do you need a ride, sweetheart?"

Grace blinks and whispers, "What did you just call me?"

"Um." Mom tilts her head, and for a second there's an awkward silence. "I just thought we could drive you home."

"Oh, uh, no. I can walk."

"It's getting dark and snowing. Where do you live?"

Excellent question, Mom.

"Not far."

"Jason, why don't you drive her home? Rourke can ride along."

"Sure. But maybe she wants to walk."

Good ol' Dad.

"You can drop me at the Elm Street gas station. Dad will be there."

"He works there?" Mom's tone makes it clear she doesn't consider working at a service station a real career for a parent.

"Only on weekends. He's looking for a second job."

Mom's eyebrows shoot up. "I see."

The idea of meeting Grace's dad makes my stomach tighten. Maybe I should ask *him* about those bruises on Grace's wrists.

I put a fistful of Mom's overdone cookies into a bag and hand them to Grace before we head out. The way Grace smiles at me—well, I'll give her cookies every day for that.

We pull up to the corner station. "There he is." Grace points to a tall man changing a tire.

When Grace hops out, her dad notices her and steps out of the garage, wiping his hands on a greasy rag.

"Hi, Dad!"

As he approaches our car, my shoulders bunch up. His arms

are muscular, and I find myself staring at his hands as he reaches in to shake hands with Dad. His youthful haircut and face surprise me, but his sagging shoulders make him look tired.

The way he pulls Grace to him makes me flinch.

"It's a pleasure to meet you. I'm Greg Elliott." His voice is strong, like his arms.

He turns to me. "And you must be the Rourke I've heard about." He crushes my hand with his vise-grip handshake. It wouldn't take much to leave a bruise with hands like his.

"Did you manage to teach Grace a few more dance moves?" I can't tell if he's accusing me of something or just making conversation.

"She's a fast learner." I try to sound normal.

"I'll expect a dance show when we go home," he says with an insistence I don't like.

"I had fun, Dad."

Mr. Elliott tightens his grip on Grace's shoulder.

"Great. Well, thanks for driving her. I understand an archery lesson is up next." He smiles, and I notice it's the same great smile as Grace's.

"So I hear," Dad says. "Grace, maybe your mom can call and reassure Rourke's mother that shooting an arrow is a safe sport."

Grace's dad gives her a questioning look. She returns it with a tight smile. Something is off.

Other than my suspicions about her dad, my whole body is smiling. Is this what it's like to have a crush on a girl?

Sam nods.

I want to text Grace to thank her for coming over, but I don't have her phone number. Even if I did, it would be dangerous to text my friends on Mom's phone.

CHAPTER 28

Don't waste today worrying about tomorrow.
~Sam

I n art class we are working on shading: dark gray, medium gray, light gray. I'm not much of an artist, but this isn't real drawing. Just shading. Kind of boring, honestly. But I love the freedom of the class because we can move around and talk to anyone as long as we're working.

Monica moves her paper and drawing pencils to my desk, then pushes her chair close to mine. Way too close. Our arms are touching.

What is she doing?

"Hi, Rourkey."

Rourkey?

"Who are you taking to the winter dance?"

"Uh... I haven't really thought about it."

She's wearing purple eye shadow and smells like peaches.

"What do you mean? It's only two weeks away!"

Why do I always sweat so bad around girls?

I concentrate on my darkest shade and go over and over it.

"I have an idea," she purrs. "You could ask me."

I clasp my pencil so hard it snaps.

My eyes dart around the room, worried someone heard her. Man, this girl's bold.

I look straight into her blue eyes and stammer, "Wh-why

aren't... How come?" I sound like an idiot. After oxygen returns to my brain, I try again. "Why aren't you going with Bart?"

"He has to go to his cousin's wedding or funeral or whatever... I'd rather go with you, anyway."

It's so hot in here. "Serious?" my voice squeaks.

"Yes." And she nudges my elbow and giggles.

My heart is pounding so hard I'm sure the whole class hears it hammering.

"Pick me up at seven." She moves her stuff back to her own desk, and the bell rings.

Unbelievable. I have a date with supermodel Monica Monahan. And knowing Monica, it's going to take all of five minutes for this to get around the school and back to Bart. He's gonna freak. I'll be a dead man. But a happy dead man. Maybe it's finally payback time for the way Bart treats Carson.

Sam grins from ear to ear.

Naturally, Monica tells everyone *I* asked *her* to the dance. Bart blows a gasket. "Stealing bases is one thing, but stealing my girlfriend has consequences, Berger."

I use a line I heard in a movie once. "We're just going as friends, Bart." I want to set him straight that Monica asked *me*, but the truth might make him madder. "If you were in town, Bart, she'd be with you. Plus, I have to keep an eye on my brother at the dance. So how much time am I gonna spend with your girlfriend?"

Never mind that Carson isn't going to the dance.

"In fact, the way I see it, Bart, I'm doing you a favor keeping her away from all the other guys who will be lining up to dance with her while *you*, my man, are out of town." I sound more confident than I am.

"Berger. I'm gonna have my posse watching you and, for your sake, I hope your 'friends' story holds up."

When I run into Phinney, he's beaming.

"Rourke-man, you're going to the dance with Monica! I'm not sure she's your type, but which magic man helped you pull this one off?"

I think the answer is Sam. He's trying just about everything to keep the worry bomb in my gut from detonating.

CHAPTER 29

Things are not always as they appear.
~Mr. Salzmann

I've been saving my giant peanut butter jar of coins to buy something special. When I notice Mr. Salzmann opening the gate to his backyard, I get an idea. Why not buy binoculars to spy on the redneck neighbors?

The bank teller pours the jar of coins into their counting machine. "Congratulations on disciplining yourself to save your money. You have $84.45. What are you planning to do with it?"

Carson is beside me and blurts out, "We're going to buy binoculars to look at hot chickens."

My ears grow warm, but the teller just laughs.

Carson has never used binoculars before. I help him adjust them and he looks at the stars, the neighbors' doorknobs, and a lot of light bulbs. We find a gap in the Salzmann's fence. Only one of the binocular lenses fits it, but it's enough to give us a glimpse of their backyard. Their beast of a dog is chained to a stake. Beside the dog, there's a huge hole dug in the ground with an eight-foot-tall hunk of wood stuck in it.

"I l-l-like being a detective with you, Rourke."

"Yeah, these neighbors are worth checking out."

The next day we hear the chainsaw and run to look through the hole, but it's been covered with a metal piece from the other side.

Busted!

For weeks, Carson and I spy on the Salzmanns and all the strange-looking people who come and go from their home. They pull up in shady-looking vans and loud motorcycles. Some stay. Others meet the old guy in the driveway and exchange packages through the car window.

One day, a guy pushing a younger man in a wheelchair catches my attention. He heads right to the Salzmann's padlocked gate, taps a code into a keypad, and opens the gate. They disappear into the garage and the gate closes. An hour later, the man who had been pushing the wheelchair drives a shiny new car out of the garage and leaves.

Mom catches me spying and lectures about using my time more wisely by emptying the dishwasher. So I empty the dishwasher, but when Mom leaves to buy groceries, I return to my perch in the dining room. The wheelchair dude and the oldest Salzmann son, Randall, have come out of the house. Randall's limping, and the guy in the wheelchair doesn't have any legs! He's holding a large metal capsule in his lap and hands an envelope to Randall. I open the window to see if I can hear them.

They pass by the flea-bitten dog-beast and Randall lifts the man in the wheelchair up into the camper. Soon, I hear muffled shouting and notice the camper rocking back and forth.

Wham!

What was that?

When I hear the bang again, I realize it's coming from our back door.

Wham! Wham! Geez. Hold on. Did Carson lock himself out? I thought he was in his room.

I run to the door with my binoculars still in my hand. I open it to find the bearded Mr. Salzmann waiting. I gasp. An old camouflaged cap is pulled tight on his head, leaving some gray and brown hair sticking out. He's a lot taller than he looks through my binoculars. Dirtier, too.

I want to move back but I'm frozen to the floor. Part of Mr. Salzmann's jaw and cheek are missing. The whole left side of his face is grotesquely sunken and discolored, and his left ear is gone. This is one guy who looks better from a distance.

The old man moves his arms out from behind his back. I sway at the sight of his chainsaw.

Mom! Dad! Sam!

CHAPTER 30

I stumble back. My mouth is sandpaper. I pray Carson stays up in his room.

"What do you want?" I croak.

He stares at my binoculars. He must know I've been spying and has come to take care of the problem. My mind races through all the ways he could do it. Starting with his chainsaw.

I push the binoculars toward him. "Here. You can have 'em."

Raising his chainsaw in front of my face, he grumbles. "That ain't what I came for."

His voice is disturbingly quiet and calm. His smoky breath drifts toward me, and I'm estimating it's been a while since he's brushed his teeth. Not that he has many to brush.

The old man isn't satisfied to take my spying tool; he's come to take me out. Maybe he thinks I've seen too much. My knees are Jell-O, and I need to pee in the worst way.

"I need to use your phone," he says, even softer than before.

You mean before or after you kill me?

"I'm not supposed to let strangers in when my parents are gone." He must hear my heart pounding.

"Your parents are gone?" he says in his hoarse voice. I swear I see a smirk tug at the corner of his mouth.

Why in the world did I say that?

"Uh, they'll be back in a few seconds." I squeak. "Can you come back then? Or better yet, I'll have them call you."

"They ain't gonna call me. My phone's out."

Oh. Right.

Hasn't this guy heard of cell phones? He's got all those fancy, expensive toys, and he's trying to tell me he doesn't own a cell?

And then there's the chainsaw. He sees me staring at it.

"Look, it's an emergency. I need a phone." There's silence as he stares a hole through me. "Please."

Oh, a polite criminal.

"And I'm *not* a stranger." He looks at my binoculars as he states this.

I motion with a stiff arm toward the last rotary wall phone in the world. As he moves toward it, I back away and escape out the door, gulping in the afternoon air.

The rough bark of the old oak tree feels good as I lean into it. By the time my pulse has slowed, another voice is inside the kitchen.

"Carson!" I rush back through the door.

Carson is kneeling beside the old man, and the chainsaw is resting on the floor between them. "What's this r-r-rope for?"

"You pull it to start the engine. And this is the chain brake used for safety."

My heart is hammering. "You're not starting that thing in here!"

Mr. Salzmann looks up. "Oh my, no. Just answering the boy's questions."

CHAPTER 31

Rourke is good at basketball. I'm good at matching keys to locks.
~Carson

After my midterm warnings, I manage to pull my grades up, but my parents aren't impressed. Three Cs, a B-, a B+ from Puddles, and an A- in math. All I know is the grades are good enough to keep me in basketball.

"My favorite part of winter is here, Mom!" I throw the basketball to her as she walks through the living room.

"Fine." She tosses it back. "But just remember, it's never basketball season in our living room."

"Mr. Piper is the coach and rumor is if you do well in his math class, which I do, then you have a decent chance of getting playing time. I don't want to spend the whole season on the bench."

"That's great, Rourke, but..." She taps my basketball and points to the hoop in our driveway.

"Oh, Mom!"

BETWEEN SCHOOL, basketball, and the usual chaos at home, the days sail by. Something's going on with my body though. Some mornings I have trouble dragging myself out of bed. Phinney keeps reminding me I'm going to the dance with the most popular girl in seventh grade, so I can't get sick now.

Speaking of the dance, I'm relieved Carson's not going. With no one (but me) there to supervise him, who knows what can happen.

Of course Mom's trying to convince him. "Carson, you should go!" She yells over the sound of the washer. "You love to dance!"

"I'm not g-g-going." Carson is sitting on the floor in the hall outside my room where I'm trying to finish math homework. His sticker bins surround him. He peels off a Batman sticker and presses it into his sticker notebook.

"You could hang out with your friends at the dance."

"Only one is going."

"Oh? Who's that?"

"Rourke."

I smile.

"Who's your other friend?"

"Peter Salzmann."

What? I look out at the Salzmann's big fence. I want Carson to have friends but not if they're weird like Peter.

"Who are you going with, Rourke?" calls Mom.

"Just Phinney." There's no way I'm telling her about my date with Monica. I don't need the momma drama.

Two days before the dance, Lucy and Eva tear up the steps and into my bedroom chanting, "Rourkey's got a girlfriend. Rourkey's got a girlfriend."

They prance around me and sing their chant over and over until I chase them out. They giggle and continue broadcasting their news down the hall.

Somehow Monica's gossip zip-line has reached my second-grade sisters. Now I have to figure out how to bribe them to keep their mouths shut so my parents don't find out. I don't need Mom lecturing me on girl stuff.

"ROURKE JASON BERGER, why didn't you tell us you asked a girl to the school dance?" Mom asks as she sets out the cereal boxes.

I shoot daggers at my sisters as I grab a granola bar. "Why can't you two mind your own business?"

"Oh, it wasn't them. Carson told us. He says she's pretty." She gives me a wink.

Carson enters the kitchen and sits down. I give him an accusing look, but I'm wasting my time as he isn't so great at reading body language—not that he's even looking at me.

"Her name is M o n i c a." Lucy exaggerates Monica's name like she's introducing a movie star.

"What's her last name?" Mom asks.

"Monroe," Carson answers.

I give Carson the *I-don't-think-so!* look and swallow a chunk of my granola bar whole which brings on a coughing fit.

"Hmmm... Monica Monroe. I don't know her. Is she new to town? What are her parents' names?"

Once I recover from coughing, I say, "I don't know but I think her sister is Marilyn."

Mom laughs. The rest don't get it.

"She's the hot chicken I spilled spaghetti on," Carson states.

"Carson!" I shout.

"The mean one?" Of course Lucy would remember this.

Always the one to try and smooth things over, Eva smiles

with her eyes sparkling. "Well, she must have liked it since she's Rourkey's girlfriend now."

"She's *not* my girlfriend. I didn't ask her to the dance. She asked me. And it's Monica *Monahan*, not Monroe!" I shove my chair back and stomp out.

Sam tries to settle me down, but I don't want to settle down. I snatch my backpack and bolt out the door. Carson can figure out how to get to school on his own. I don't care how many buses run him over.

Monroe! Where did he pull that one from?

Phinney listens to me boil over for a couple blocks.

"Sorry, Phin. I'm not sure why I'm carrying on about the whole Monica thing."

"I bet you do. I think the reason sits right in front of you in math."

Phinney's right. I could kick myself for not asking Grace to the dance.

CHAPTER 32

Can I trust Rourke with a secret?
~Grace

My legs are heavy. I drag myself to math class. What's wrong with me? Maybe I need more sleep.

Grace smiles at me as I walk in, and I forget about my tired body. If she knew I was taking Monica to the dance, I doubt she'd even look at me.

Today she has on a gray and blue sweater with sleeves rolled up a couple times but long enough to still cover her wrists. I don't spend much time scoping out girls' clothes, but it seems like a lot of Grace's clothes are too big for her. Maybe it's the new look.

She twists her body around and asks, "When do you want your archery lesson?"

"Are you kidding? We have two feet of snow. If I shot an arrow you'd never find it until spring."

She giggles, which makes her eyes twinkle. "First of all, we don't have much snow and second, you're not going to miss the target once you get a lesson from me."

"Oh, I get it. You're going to reverse three weeks of Puddles' instruction, which I apparently flunked, in one fell swoop."

"Yep!" Her lips curve up.

"I wouldn't bet on that. In fact, if you can get me to hit even one bullseye at your place, I'll..."

"Take me to a movie?"

What? This girl is full of surprises.

I laugh. "Oh, I get it. You have ulterior motives for teaching me how to shoot."

"With popcorn?" Her eyes widen as she waits for my answer.

I guess the girls make the dates in this school.

"Actually *extra-large* popcorn with a drink?" She tilts her head for emphasis.

"Now you're getting greedy."

"No. Just making sure you want to learn how to shoot better."

What would she think if I said I didn't really care about archery? That I just want to hang out with her.

"I can bike over Sunday." A wave of nausea washes over me. The thought of biking exhausts me.

Now she'll have to tell me where she lives. First she said she was moving and then it was "near Manley Wood." That's definitely not near the golf course, so maybe her house is a palace on a country estate.

"You bike in the winter?"

I shake my head to clear the fog. "Yep. My bike has fat tires to grip snow."

"You know where the blue water tower is? Meet me there at one and we can walk to where I keep my bow."

She has a place where she keeps her bow?

"Wait a sec. I have to volunteer this weekend. How about next Sunday? Rourke?"

"Yeah. Oh, sorry. Yeah. Next Sunday works." I catch myself as my elbow that is supporting my chin slips.

"Are you all right?"

"I'm fine." The Berger mantra.

IN THE EVENING Grandma Penny calls and insists I bike over and try to beat her in double solitaire. My legs shake when I get off my bike.

Grandma easily wins a couple rounds.

"Grandma, did you ever make a decision you regretted?"

She laughs. "Only about every day." Grandma looks at me closer and frowns. "Rourke, what's the matter? You look pale."

If Grandma is noticing, I must look bad.

"Here, have a cookie. In fact, have two. I'll get you a glass of milk. And remember, Rourke, regret is a waste of time. Saying you're sorry isn't."

CHAPTER 33

I try not to think too far ahead about Carson's future.
~Mrs. Berger

It's school dance night. I hold up a shirt from my drawer. Is this a middle school dance shirt? It's plaid. It's got that stuffed-in-a-drawer wrinkled look. Perfect.

I put it on and think about Grace. She found out last week I'm going with Monica to the dance and hasn't talked to me since. Should I bother telling her Monica pretty much told me I was taking her? Would Grandma's advice to say "I'm sorry" work?

I look at myself in the mirror. The shirt is a little small. I find another one with the same wrinkled look. Am I supposed to look like I'm working at impressing Monica? There must be books on this stuff, like *Middle School Dressing for Dummies*.

I switch from jeans to khakis and back to jeans. And add deodorant. Lots.

Sam watches me tap my fingers on the bed and tries to tell me school dances are fun. I focus on fun until Mom comes into my room and breaks the news. "Carson's going to the dance! Won't he love it?"

I didn't have the energy to convince Mom that my first school dance date shouldn't include a third wheel.

At seven sharp, Dad drives me to Monica's house to pick her up. If I had an x-ray of my stomach, I know I'd see one huge knot. I wait in her entryway, making small talk with her mother. When she comes downstairs, I can't help but think she resembles Marilyn Monroe with all her makeup and blonde hair.

As Monica climbs in the back seat, she notices my brother. "Oh, hi Carson. Are you coming to the dance too?"

"Yes, I am. Are you going?"

"I sure am! We're all going to have a blast."

God bless Monica for her kindness.

Dad winks at me when he drops the three of us off at the front door of the middle school.

Puddles and Nicotine Nancy are event supervisors and hold the doors open for us. Phinney and Maggie meet us just inside. I look at Phinney's clothes. "What in the world?" He tips his safari hat at me and grins.

As I hang up Monica's jacket, I can't believe it's me she chose as her stand-in for Bart. I look at her as she waits for me by the gym door. It seems she's had another trip to the mall. She's wearing a lacey thing over a shimmery blue dress. Does she realize we live in Hazard, Indiana, not Hollywood? I doubt she's even looked at *my* clothes, which is probably a good thing.

I look around for Carson. Hopefully he doesn't run off and get lost.

Sam interrupts my thoughts. *Carson's fine. This is your chance to dance and relax with friends.*

Monica grabs my arm and pulls me into the gym. When I see her glossy-lipped smile, I am no longer Rourke Berger. Maybe Justin Bieber.

The gym is dark except for the exit lights and the D.J. equipment. The flashing of a strobe light disorients me for a few seconds, as does a twirling mirrored ball hanging from the ceiling. All this and pulsating music has transformed Mr. Presell's gym into a dance club!

Once my eyes adjust I look around and notice Miss Thompson in the corner. She waves, making me a bit self-conscious.

The D.J. is playing Katy Perry's "Firework." Monica drags me onto the dance floor where everyone sings along.

A connection floats into my head over the song lyrics...a house of cards...one blow from caving in.

Sam scolds me. *Stop it! This is a night to have fun!*

There's a big crowd on the dance floor, and Phinney is the center of attention. He's dressed as part safari hunter, part leopard, and dances like a wild animal that's just been let out of a cage. He pounces toward other kids and roars, causing everyone else to roar.

"Play the Macarena!" someone yells. The D.J. obliges. Puddles joins us, and other teachers get into it too, including Mad Marlys. She may be old, but she can still move it.

After a half hour we take a break. Monica runs off to the girls' room with a half dozen of her fan club, and I head to the cafeteria with Phinney.

"Phin-man, you look like you robbed the Goodwill store!"

"I call this my chick-magnet look!" he says with a smirk. As Phinney and I have a soda, I can't stop smiling, until I turn around.

Carson is sitting at a table by himself on the far side of the cafeteria. My heart sinks. Is he going to sit there all night alone? There's nothing wrong with going over to make sure he's okay.

Sam suggests that maybe Carson likes being alone.

Phinney calls out, "Rourke-man, I'm heading back to the gym. I gotta teach those girls more of my moves!" I give him the thumbs up before I turn back to Carson.

A girl sits down and talks to him. My stomach dips. I can only see the back of her, but I'd know that hair from a mile away.

I watch Carson and Grace with a great deal of curiosity. I've never seen him alone with a girl before. Grace pushes her chair back and walks to the concession stand. I stop in my tracks as my jaw drops open. Wow! She's in a dress.

I move closer.

Grace brings Carson a couple slices of pepperoni pizza—his favorite—and an orange crush, the only soda he'll drink. The Girl Scout is back on duty.

They laugh over something, like friends do. I can't stand it. I'm going over there.

"Hey, Carson! Having some pizza?"

"S-s-starving. This girl and I are eating." Carson takes a huge bite, letting pizza sauce drip down his chin.

"Hi, Grace," I try to sound friendly but she's not buying it. Her eyes narrow as she bites into her pizza. It's obvious she's seen me with Monica by now. I'm a hypocrite and deserve this, but it bothers me when she won't even look my way.

I sit down beside Carson, which means I'm right across from Grace. "Can you believe how packed this place is?"

Sam is in my ear. *This is your chance to make up with her.*

Grace shifts in her chair and has eyes only for her pizza. Maybe I'll leave and let her go back to entertaining Carson.

An arm wraps around my neck. "There you are, Rourkey! Are you gonna buy me something to drink? All that dancing with you has made me *so* thirsty!"

Monica and her friends surround me with loud giggles.

Embarrassed, I stand up. "Uh, sure."

"Well hello, Gretchen!" Monica calls to Grace, spreading the fake friendliness on way too thick. "What are *you* doing here?"

Grace winces and pushes her chair back.

"Her name's Grace," I say.

Monica ignores me and continues, "Don't you have

something better to do tonight—like squirrel hunting with your bow and arrow?"

Oh boy. Mean girl.

Grace jumps up as if she's ready to claw Monica's eyes out, and that's when I notice fresh purple bruises on her left forearm.

"Hey!" Carson shouts. "You're the hot chicken I dropped my spaghetti on."

Unbelievable! Carson rode in the same car with Monica and me to this dance and he said nothing. Now he suddenly recognizes her?

I risk a peek at Monica. If looks could kill, Carson would be long gone. As Monica grabs my arm and hauls me toward the concession stand, Grandma Penny's advice floods my brain. I turn and say, "I'm sorry!" Grace doesn't look like she believes me.

Monica and I share a slice of pizza and a soda. Phinney bumps up against me and mutters, "That's almost like sharing smooches, Rourke-man."

We go back into the gym, where I try to forget about Carson and Grace. Monica screams as the electric slide begins. "I love this dance!" She bounces up and down to the rhythm.

The steps we learned in Puddles' dance class come back to me. Backward, forward, turn. I laugh when Phinney turns in the wrong direction and tries to correct himself. Maggie's eyes twinkle as she bumps into him.

I exchange a silly look with Monica as we jump and move with the music. Tension slides off my body and evaporates.

The next dance is a slow one. Monica's thrilled, but this is the moment I've dreaded. I've never done this before except in dance class, and that was only because Puddles told us it was part of the state standards.

I seriously need more deodorant.

It seems like every girl in the place screams and gasps like they're going to hyperventilate. Most go running off the gym floor and sit down to watch the "slow dance" couples. This is all new and strange to me, but kind of exciting, like I'm a mini-celebrity.

Monica takes control. She turns to face me, grabs my left hand in her right one and puts her left arm up on my right shoulder. She's done this before. The only place for my right arm is around her waist.

Then a miracle happens. Monica stops talking. A slow-dance shuts her up. I'll have to remember that.

The words of the song are pretty sappy. Something about someone loving you forever. The scent of Monica's hair distracts me from the rest of the words. It smells like strawberries. She moves in closer and lays her head on my shoulder. This is all new and awkward and nice. I try to stay off her feet. And then for some reason, Bart flies into my brain.

I haven't thought of him all night, but now I picture him coming back early. What if he comes crashing in here and flips out when he sees me slow dancing to a song about loving his girlfriend forever? A chill goes down my spine as I eye the double doors.

No Bart in sight. Just Carson. Beside him is Grace, looking like she's taken her archery stance and is ready to shoot. I watch her from the dark dance floor.

The music skips and the D.J. apologizes for the technical problem and lets the song start over. Then, something weird happens. Carson awkwardly puts his arms around Grace, and they dance. Slow, not moving much. He's actually touching somebody. A girl. *My* Girl Scout!

I step back from Monica. "I need a drink." I don't really, but I have to talk to Grace right now.

Sam warns me that Grace isn't ready to talk yet.

I walk to the door, but only Carson is there. "Where did Grace go?"

"I want to dance," Carson says.

"Did Grace leave?"

"Who's Grace?"

"Grace! Grace Elliott. You know, the girl who bought you pizza and soda? You were just dancing with her!"

"I don't know. Can I dance with you?"

I growl as the gym floor literally bounces. The "Y.M.C.A." song has started. As long as you can get your body to form those four letters—shoot, even if you can't—everyone is happy.

Carson is still begging. "Puhleeeez dance with me!"

I grab Carson's arm, laughing. "Let's go, bro!"

Watching Carson on the dance floor takes me back to the silly things we used to do together. He's kind of a goofy dancer, but so am I. He twirls me around, high-fives the girls, and looks, well…like the rest of us.

My Carson moment ends as someone requests another slow song, and naturally, Monica drags me away from Carson. As I'm thinking of how to escape to find Grace before she gets away, I notice Carson standing in the middle of the dance floor. His body is rigid, his arms are locked at his sides with fists balled, and his eyes are fixed on the strobe light.

No! Not again!

CHAPTER 34

I notice everything—it's like watching thirty TV channels all at once.
~Carson

"Carson!"

I push Monica so hard she stumbles and slides on her bottom.

The earth shifts. The weight of it crushes me. I manage to race around all the couples on the floor like I'm sashaying down a ski slope, nearly taking some of them out as I cut corners too close.

Panic-stricken, I scream, "Turn 'em off. Turn the strobe lights off!" The music drowns me out.

By the time I make it to him, Carson has dropped to the floor, his limbs shaking. His eyes are rolled back, and the sight of it sucks the life from me. So much for the seizure medicine.

I take hold of his arms, but they feel mechanical, like they're locked. Nausea rises as the knot in my gut cinches tighter. Something jolts my brain, and I reach into my pocket for the cell phone.

I have to try the password three times before my shaky fingers get it right, then I hit "home" on the favorites list. It seems like an eternity before Dad answers. "It's Carson. Another seizure I think. Hurry Dad, please hurry."

By now, the music has stopped and everyone but the teachers has run for the hills.

Carson grinds his teeth, and I cringe, longing for Katy Perry's sweet voice or even Monica's incessant chatter to drown out the sound.

The adults surround us, and Mr. Allen, the assistant principal, kneels beside me. "Rourke, what do you do when this happens?"

What do I do? Can't you see? I scream. Part of me dies. That's what I do.

Carson stops thrashing and coils into a fetal position.

"Oh, no!" I yell. "I don't think he's breathing."

I bend over Carson, rub his back and rock back and forth. I pray and cry and gasp for my own breath, choking out his name over and over.

"Sam! Someone help—please!" Panic is squeezing the life from my lungs.

Where are Mom and Dad, for Pete's sake? And Sam! You gotta help me!

The gym lights slowly come up, which gives me a better look at Carson's face. His face and lips look blue. "Don't die on me! Don't do this! Don't leave me, buddy!" I scream. I lose sight of him through my tears and rest my face on his chest.

Somewhere in the distance I hear Miss Thompson on her phone asking questions about seizures.

Mr. Allen tries to pull me back. "I'll start CPR."

But I won't let go. "No, he's having a seizure. You're not supposed to do CPR!" I scream. I let myself drown in fear for some unending amount of time as my heart shakes in my chest.

Miraculously, Carson moves beneath me. I half laugh and half cry between hysteria and the horrific reality of it all.

Someone touches me again. I react with a jolt and rear back.

"Rourke. It's Dad. We're here."

"Finally!" I turn and collapse in his arms, almost knocking him over. I clutch his shirt as I rock, and gasp, and fight for sanity.

"He's okay. Carson's coming around." Mom pulls me off Dad so he can tend to Carson.

I suck in air as my lungs start functioning again and bawl in my mother's arms like a baby.

I WAKE the following morning with a mega headache. I had another nightmare but don't even try to remember what it was. The one I'll never forget is the one in the gym.

After a long shower, I sit on my bed and stare into space until I hear Mom.

"I made some blueberry muffins."

I can't look at her. How do parents survive this parenting thing? How do they just get up after a night like last night and make muffins?

I follow Mom downstairs and slide into a kitchen chair. She's calm, matter-of-fact, and takes a bite of her muffin.

"We're having Carson go through some testing. Some people with autism have seizures, but there's medicine to control them." She hands me a muffin.

I take a bite. My mouth is so dry I can barely swallow. "Will we have to pay for the mirrored ball thing?"

"Maybe. You really hammered it."

I can't tell if she's angry or impressed.

Last night, I waited for the disco ball to be lowered from the ceiling. Together with the pulsating strobe light, that mirrored creature ruined my first school dance. Carson's too.

I had pulled a bat from a bin of gym equipment. *Perfect,* I remember thinking. I walked to the demonic ball, gave it one solid whack, and returned the bat to the bin. No one said a thing. Mr. Allen helped the custodian clean it up, like it was all in a day's work at Hazard Middle School.

Mom sets her coffee cup down. "It's my fault," she whispers through quivering lips. "He didn't want to go. I made him." She holds her head in her hands and cries.

It's one thing for me to lose control, but when my mother breaks down, my worry-meter shoots off the chart.

CHAPTER 35

There are 102 windows in the houses on our cul-de-sac.
~Carson

I hand Grace a note in math.

G. Are we still on for archery Sunday? R.

When the dismissal bell rings at the end of math, Grace shoots daggers at me. It looks like her answer is *no*.

Maybe "I'm sorry" wasn't enough.

AFTER DINNER, I try reading my *Mockingbird* assignment, but I keep nodding off. The cover is coated with Carson's stickers, as he got the idea to "decorate" my book.

Nicotine Nancy is into this book, and it's not bad, but it's hard to concentrate when I'm so tired. I swear I'm dragging an extra hundred pounds around. Mom notices when she stops in my room.

"Rourke, you have dark circles under your eyes and you aren't eating much these days. Are you feeling okay?"

Like a truck ran over me. A truck named worry. "I'm fine, Mom."

"Let's take your temperature."

She comes back with the thermometer and my sisters. "Hmm...it's normal."

"Maybe he's lovesick," Eva suggests.

Mom smiles. "And Dr. Berger, how did you come up with this diagnosis?"

"He misses Grace."

Mom nods. "You should invite her over again, Rourke. I like her."

I lie back onto my bed.

"I'm making an appointment for you to see Dr. Peterson. You never know what might be going around."

Like a brother who nearly dies in your arms. Is there medicine for that?

SATURDAY MORNING the phone rings while I'm doing some math homework. Dad picks it up downstairs. His voice moves from the kitchen to the office. I'm sure he's stretching the cord far enough so he can sit down at the desk.

Dad, please ditch the cord phones!

I plug music in my ears.

Dad calls up the stairway a couple minutes later. "Rourke, come down here please."

I pretend I don't hear. I'm sure he wants me to babysit or collect trash.

"*Rourke!*"

"Yeah. Fine. I'll be down when I get this math done." I glance out the window. Some snow flurries but nothing serious. No chance of having a snow day off of school at this rate. I could use a day to sleep in.

When I go downstairs, Dad's in Mom's office drawing cartoons—his favorite pastime. He stands when I come in and runs his hands through his hair. It's his sign for "someone's in trouble."

"Son, have a seat."

Son? He never calls me that. Unless I'm in trouble.

"Gramps just called."

I sigh with relief.

He looks out the window. Then across at me. He's stalling. "Son."

Okay, that's twice. Something's up.

"It's Grandma Penny." He takes a deep breath and takes forever to let it out. "She had a massive stroke this morning."

I tense. "What's that mean?"

"It means blood flow to the brain gets cut off and there is swelling of the brain."

I jump up. "Well, let's go see her! Is she in the hospital?"

"No, Rourke. I'm sorry. She's... gone."

Gone? As in dead? That can't be right!

"No, I just saw her yesterday. We played chess. She..." I clutch the chair to keep from passing out. I sit again and lean forward to support my head.

Dad wraps himself around me but I push back. Grandma's dead? I break away and run to my room. Rocking back and forth on my bed in misery, I gasp loud breathy cries until my body is stripped of energy.

"HERE. I forgot to give you this yesterday." Carson drops a piece of wadded-up paper on my chest.

I knock it to the floor. I can't deal with his little games today. Grandma Penny is dead.

Carson puts his hand to my forehead the way Mom does to check our temperature. "You look sicker than a dog."

I turn my eyes to Carson and chuckle. Carson just used an

idiom. You look sicker than a dog. Almost a joke. Not that he was trying to make one.

Carson leaves the room, and I sit up on my bed. I kick the crumpled piece of paper back and forth between my feet and finally pick it up. I flatten it out and see a miracle.

Sunday 1:00. GS

I'VE ONLY BEEN to one funeral, when Dad's cousin died. I was only six and didn't know June Collins. I hadn't seen her smile, never heard her voice. If she had hobbies or favorite food, I didn't know what they were.

And when you're six, you don't think as much about what it means when people die. I remember a bunch of people crying though, and it made me wonder why Mom and Dad would haul their little kids to such a sad affair when they wouldn't even let us watch movies where animals died.

Grandma's funeral is different. This is someone I loved, and I'm not six anymore. I know where she kept her secret candy stash. She anticipated my moves in chess. In fact, she just beat me seven days ago.

After the service we're ushered into a dining area to eat. As I take a bite, I see someone sitting alone across the room. She's facing the wall so I only see her back. But it's enough.

Why is Grace here? Is she playing Girl Scout and volunteering at funerals?

My attention is pulled back when I hear Mom crying. Gramps reaches for Mom's hand and strokes it. Then he turns to me. "Rourke. Grandma told me you talked to her about your pretend friend."

I freeze.

"She said he gives you advice on how to stop worrying."

I don't dare look at my parents. What will they think of their almost teen-aged kid having an imaginary friend? I turn to where Grace had been sitting. She's gone.

I dread the ride home.

Mom doesn't ask any questions. Not directly.

"Grandma was lucky to have you in her life, Rourke. She loved it when you came over and helped her with her chores and played games... and talked. You have a knack for helping others. That's a gift."

My armpits drip as I stare out the window.

"But it's okay for you to get help sometimes, too."

She thinks I'm crazy.

CHAPTER 36

We all need distractions.
~Grace

From a block away I see her blue jacket. Grace is already at the water tower even though I'm early. The butterflies are back. As curious as I am about a girl who can shoot a perfect arrow, I'm even more curious about how she can forgive a jerk like me, so I brought a couple apples and a package of store-bought cookies as a peace offering.

"Hi," she calls out.

At least she's talking.

"Hey. Where's your bike?"

"We sold it before we moved here. It wouldn't work for me in the snow anyway. I don't know how you ride in it."

I hop off and walk along beside her. Smiling, I say, "I guess we all have our strengths."

She grins. "Maybe I shouldn't teach you my archery tricks so I can be better than you at one thing."

Whew, she hasn't lost her sense of humor.

"Are we going to your house to shoot arrows?"

"No, just an old barn where I practice."

"You have a barn?"

"It belongs to a guy my dad works for."

"I have to call my mom and let her know where we are. You

know how mothers are. They want to know where you are at all times in case of some national emergency like telling you it's dinner time."

Grace frowns. "You shouldn't give your mom such a hard time."

Okay. I was just making a little joke.

We walk to the edge of town.

"How's Carson doing?"

"He's seeing a doctor to find out what's up."

"And you?"

I ponder how to answer her and settle on, "I'm fine."

She stops walking and looks at me. "No, you're not."

Her words stop me in my tracks.

"Neither am I," she continues. "That's why I shoot. To forget about family stuff."

I trail after her to a weathered looking barn with a boarded up window. "You're right about it being old."

"Yeah. I suppose it used to be red, but it has character now."

The overhead track groans as Grace heaves the sliding door open. When we get inside she switches on a light and shoves the door shut again.

I lean my bike against the wall. It's a neat old place with pigeons cooing on the rafters. Straw bales are stacked against the opposite wall. I take a deep breath. The sweet smell settles into me. "Cool!"

She grins and nods in agreement.

A ray of dusty sunlight streams in, casting a spotlight on the archery target standing in front of the bales.

"Wow. This place is like a magazine picture."

"I wouldn't go that far, but I like it."

Grace disappears into a tiny space complete with cobwebs and comes out with a bow and a bag of arrows.

"I'm going to show you what you were doing wrong in Presell's class."

"Wrong?" I exaggerate my shock.

"Yeah. You grip the bow so darn tight with your left hand," she says. "When you release the arrow, the muscles in your hand relax and it throws off the direction of the arrow."

"Grace."

She keeps talking as though she didn't hear me call her name. "The same with your left shoulder, neck, and back. You gotta keep them relaxed, or the power released in those muscles can cause your arrow to go off target."

"Grace!"

Finally she stops.

"I wanted to take you to the dance but Monica had already asked me."

"I know."

"You knew?"

"Yep."

"Oh. And..."

"And," she grins, "now we're here, and I'm gonna help you shoot better."

After a lot of advice and attempts, I do improve. "Bullseye!" I shout when I finally get my first one.

"All right! Now you have to take me to the movies!" Her eyes shine.

"And buy you popcorn too, right?"

"An extra-large with extra butter!" Her voice sounds like a happy little kid, and I can't help but laugh.

After twenty minutes and a few more perfect shots, I take a breather. "Your turn. Show me how the experts do it."

"The experts don't use that kind of bow."

Of course not.

"And by the way, you got five bullseyes. You now owe me five movie nights."

"Oh really? Well, I better get a job first to pay for all these movies I'm taking you to."

Grace returns to the dusty closet and comes out with a strange black piece of equipment in her hand.

"*This* is my bow. It's a compound bow with decent speed and accuracy for a kid's bow."

"*That's* a kid's bow?" I gasp.

"Want to try it?" She hands it to me, but I don't know where to grab it.

"Whoa! It's heavy."

"Not really, just a few pounds."

"So call me weak!"

She giggles.

"Where did you get this thing?" I stare at its parts and can't believe Grace is into this.

"Dad gave it to me last year for Christmas."

"Why?"

"So I could hunt with him."

"Hunt?"

"Uh-huh. It's fun!"

"What do you hunt?"

"Bears."

"*What?*"

She doubles over with laughter.

"Very funny. No, really, who uses this bow?"

"Oh, I wasn't kidding. It's mine, and I do hunt, but not bears." She giggles again. "Just squirrels and rabbits. Sometimes Dad takes me deer hunting."

"Do you eat them?"

"Sometimes."

Of course she wouldn't hunt just for fun.

I sit down on a bale of straw, and she sits on another one a few feet away. "Show me." I hand the bow to her.

"It's too powerful to shoot in here."

"Oh." There's an awkward silence. "Hey." I suck in a deep breath and let it out in small bursts. "Can I ask you something?"

She shrugs. "You want to know where I live."

Yes, I want to know where she lives and why she stores food like a pack rat in her locker and what the bruises are all about, but one thing at a time...

I look across the distance between us and can't read her. "No. Something else."

She looks relieved. "What?"

"What were you doing at the funeral?"

Her head turns toward me and she wrinkles her forehead. "Huh?"

"I saw you eating at the church—after the funeral."

Her face flushes pink and she bites her lower lip.

"Whose funeral?"

She didn't know whose funeral she was at?

"My grandma's."

"Oh no, I'm sorry. When was it? The funeral, I mean."

I can't help but laugh even though none of this is funny. "Yesterday. You were there so you should know!" I don't mean to sound accusing but, come on...

"I-I didn't see you." She looks like a cornered mouse.

"Why were you there?"

"I-uh-I, was...eating."

Duh.

"I know, but were you volunteering or something?" I sound like my mother. Cross-examining her.

She gets up and fiddles with the arrow she's holding. "No. Not exactly."

"So what exactly were you doing there?"

"I didn't know it was your grandmother's funeral." She picks up another arrow and sits down again, only further away.

The silence is louder than anything I can say. Sunlight hits her hair just right, making it shine a reddish color. I can't keep my eyes off her. She's so pretty. *And lying.*

"Well, it sure wasn't McDonald's. Why were you..." I stop when she flinches. "Never mind. Look, maybe I should head ho–"

"I get hungry." She blurts it out. It doesn't sound like the usual calm and confident Grace.

What?

Her eyes are glued to the barn floor. "I eat at a lot of funerals." Her words come tumbling out.

You're joking. That's like...morbid.

"I have nothing to eat on the weekends."

My mind flashes back to Grace eyeing the lasagna and pie at my house. And all those cookies. The locker stash.

It's dead quiet, and her eyes are still locked on the floor. Finally, she takes a quick peek in my direction like she's checking to see if I've flown the coop. "At school I get free meals." Her voice is an icy whisper.

I get it. Her family is poor, and she's embarrassed.

"Grace, I'm sorry. You don't have to tell me this."

"We don't have a refrigerator."

A squeezing sensation in my head and gut threaten my ability to stand. I hold up my hand like a traffic cop to get her to stop.

"Or stove."

She's kidding.

"Or... house," she finishes.

No way. She doesn't volunteer at the homeless shelter. She lives there.

She takes deep breaths in an attempt to keep from losing it. *No, don't cry. I don't know what to do with a crying girl.*

"Where do you sleep? Where do your mom and dad and you...live? Everybody's gotta live somewhere."

This sends her. She leaps to her feet and lunges at me. Her eyes are dark and accusing and...wild.

She starts in, her piercing voice pushing me back. "I'm not everybody, am I?"

One hand is holding the arrows over her head with the sharp points toward me.

I shouldn't have come here.

"Not like the rest of your friends and you with your nice houses and perfect little families."

"Grace, my family isn't perfect."

She's still got the hunting bow in her other hand and is waving it around in exasperation. I lean back. She's scaring me.

"We don't have beds!" she yells. "And you keep asking me where I live. Well, we don't live *anywhere*." She gulps in air and thrashes her arms around, like there's no other way to get through to me but to shove it down my throat.

"We just sleep wherever they will let us park our trailer. And, and..." She's trying to keep the volume up but it's not working. What remains is a pathetic choking sound that rips me in two.

She heaves both arrows with all her might. I duck and hear them connect with the wall behind me. Holding my arms up to defend myself, I yell. "Stop it! Stop it, Grace!"

Her shoulders sag.

Her face is red and twisted in a painful way and she no longer looks thirteen. She looks older. Way older. Her eyes are flooded as she reveals her deepest sorrow. "There is no mother. She's...dead."

I catch her as she collapses in an awkward heap on the floor.

There it is, the answers to my questions—most of them, anyway.

Eating funeral meals. Hunting. No mother. What a beautiful mess she is. I guess this isn't the proper time to ask about those bruises. Crazy how a minute ago we were having so much fun. Crazy.

She lies on the floor with her head on my knee until her sobs turn to sniffles and her breathing is regular. "I'm fine now."

I will never believe that line for as long as I live.

Grace sits up, wiping her nose. Her face is red and those pretty eyes are puffy and sad. A Girl Scout, out to save the world when it's her who needs saving.

We both stand, and she picks up her hunting bow. I collect the arrows, including the ones stuck in the wall, and hand the wimpy bow to her so she can put it away.

If I were an adult I might say, "Shouldn't we talk about this?" But I'm just a kid and don't even know how to handle my own problems. I have more questions for her, but I'm not sure I want to know anything else.

I push my bike outside, and Grace closes the door.

"Sorry about all that."

She's apologizing? I should be the one apologizing—for asking too many questions, for the life she has, for not asking her to the dance.

"I had no idea. You look like any other kid."

Only better.

"I am like any other kid."

With no mother, and a dad who—

I hand her the cookies and apples. She tucks them in her backpack, and we walk back toward the water tower together.

"Thanks for the shooting tips." It's lame, but all I can offer.

She tries a smile. "See you in math tomorrow."

"I'll bring you some more cookies."

Grace shrugs and attempts a smile. "I'll bring you a dead rabbit." She waves and walks away.

My energy to pedal is gone. I get off and push my bike. A minute down the road, I stop and look in the direction Grace is walking. The trailer court is not over there. She's headed toward the landfill. What hasn't she told me?

CHAPTER 37

Change is hard.
~Carson

Christmas break is finally here, and I can't wait to sleep in. I leave my overhead fan on so it covers up family "noise." Unfortunately, the fan doesn't prevent morning visitors. Around seven, Carson crashes into my room.

"Where are my stickers? Did you take them? Where are they?"

I don't answer so he shakes my shoulder and keeps at it. "What did you do with them?"

Now I'm peeved, so I throw my elbow into him.

"Ouch! You hurt me," he whimpers.

"Carson, I didn't take anything. Go ask Lucy and Eva," I mumble.

"I can't find my stickers." He rummages through my desk drawers and makes a mess, leaving them hanging open.

He climbs over my bed and shouts, "Give them back!"

"Get out!" I demand with as much energy as I can muster this early.

"I want them back!" He kicks my bed and howls over his sore foot.

Is this the way my break's gonna be? I cover my head with my pillow.

I hear Carson open my closet door and rifle through my stuff. "Can I have these?"

I don't answer.

He leaves, and later I find out he took my shoebox of baseball cards and mixed them in with his sticker collection that he eventually found in his room under a pile of his clothes. I blow a gasket. "Dad, he's taking my stuff!"

Since the college kids have gone home for the holidays, Dad is actually home for a few days. "Carson said he asked."

"Well I sure didn't say *yes*. He can't come into my room anymore. Dad, you need to tell him!"

"Do you even care about those baseball cards anymore, Rourke?"

I cannot believe what I'm hearing.

Frustrated, I grit my teeth. "Dad, you're letting Carson get away with murder here. Today he's stealing my baseball cards, tomorrow he'll be taking stickers from some store. I doubt the police will ask the store owners, 'Do you even care about those stickers Carson stole?'"

I turn to storm off, but not before saying, "I better have every one of my cards back in my closet by noon. In order. By team."

Dad's eyes grow as big as saucers. I can't believe I just said that to him, but Sam gives me the thumbs up as I stomp back to my room.

Maybe I shouldn't have barked at Dad, but my cards are back in my closet on time and in order before noon.

"Rourke, I'm sorry for what I said about your cards. I have a ton of junk I save and haven't looked at in twenty-five years, but I can't seem to give it up," Dad says.

"Oh yeah, like what?" I'm on my bed tossing a cushy ball up over my head.

"Oh, where do I start? My erector set I got when I was eight and all my college textbooks molding in the basement."

"And all your broken remote planes. Maybe we're related to the hoarders."

Dad laughs and comes over and gives me his wrestling hug. "I love Carson to pieces. I just wish..." His voice cracks.

My eyes fill, and I hold him tight. I want to say, "Me too, Dad."

"It's Christmas." His voice sounds fragile. "Let's have a peaceful one."

*W*HAM! *Wham! Wham!*

Holy smokes. What in the world? It's been less than twenty-four hours since the last forced entry and here we go again.

I was sleeping hard. Not even one nightmare. I hear Carson's voice and the doorknob to my bedroom being worked over.

"Let me in!"

Wham! Wham! He's pounding my door. Killing it.

"Carson. Stop it. You can't come in," I mumble into my pillow.

"Y-y-you can't lock doors. It's the law. You're in trouble, Rourke Berger!"

Me? Right.

Yes, it's against the law to lock bedroom doors in our house. Something about safety and gaining access in a fire or another emergency...like when someone wants to steal your baseball cards. I locked my door last night before bed and now this.

BOOM!

I bolt from my bed. Carson has kicked clean through my

door. His bare foot is inside my room, sticking out through the gaping hole. Splintered wood is scattered on the carpet.

"Owwwwww!"

I'm looking at a morning nightmare. Mom is going to freak out over the busted door.

"Carson! Are you all right?" I race to the door and attempt to push Carson's foot back through the hole but slivers poke him and he howls louder.

"Stop killing me!"

I unlock my door and pull it open, which is a mistake. The inward motion of the door pulls Carson off balance from the foot he is standing on and he falls to the floor. He tries pulling his foot out, which causes the splinters to dig deeper into his skin.

Carson screams bloody murder. And speaking of blood, there's some of that, too.

Mom bounds up the steps two at a time, followed by Dad, my sisters, and both dogs. My parents gasp and glare at me like it's my fault. Beulah licks Carson's face even though he's howling and flailing his arms around like a madman defending himself from killer bees. It's as if we're in some kind of comedy show.

Lucy giggles as she hugs the bawling Carson. And what Lucy does, Eva does. Mom and Dad both laugh hysterically—it's like we've all gone crazy. I have to sit down, I'm laughing so hard. The twins roll on the hallway floor until Lucy declares she's wet her pants. This sends us all roaring again, except Carson, who is lying on his back wailing with his bloody foot still stuck through my door.

WE GO to Gramps's for Christmas Eve dinner. Grandma Penny's empty chair stares at me, and the meatballs taste funny. After dinner we head to Christmas Eve services. Our family has a rough history of church-going. There was a long stretch when Carson couldn't sit still. One time, when Dad got mad and threatened to duct-tape him to the pew, Carson stood up and yelled, "I hate my dad!" right in the middle of Pastor Tim's sermon on honoring your father and mother.

The last time I was in a church was for Grandma's funeral. This makes me think of Grace and wonder where she is tonight. I look around, half expecting to see her. But then again, there's no food being served, unless you count the stale communion wafers.

The candlelight service is a tense ordeal. Eva isn't paying attention to how high her flame is getting and singes her hair. Carson insists on having his own candle. I offer to share my candle with him so I can control the drip, but he doesn't go for it. Gramps's pants end up with a little wax on them, but he just shrugs it off. Mom looks relieved when "Silent Night" is over and we blow out the candles.

Dad whispers to Mom, "Merry Christmas sweetheart. We've made it another year without burning the Hazard Methodist Church down."

Snow is lightly falling as we exit the church. It's like we're inside one of Grandma's snow globes. The church bells are chiming "O Holy Night" and I'm hoping Grace has something to eat. After all, it's Christmas Eve.

CHRISTMAS DAY at our house is all about eating too much and, of course, presents.

"C-c-come upstairs and see what I made you." Carson's

hands are flapping when he says this so I can tell he's excited. He's patched the hole in my door with a homemade sign.

ROURKE'S ROOM. NO TRESPASSING.

I try a fist bump with Carson but he misses, so I slap him on the shoulder instead. Sam stamps his approval, giving me more energy than I've felt in a while.

In the afternoon, Mom and I deliver Christmas cookies to Greenleaf Retirement Center. "Mom, can we drop by Grace's Dad's work with some cookies?"

"Sounds like a wonderful idea, but how about we drop them at her house?"

"I think she's volunteering today."

Mom is a saint for not asking more questions and for not grilling me about my imaginary friend.

When we return from delivering cookies I take a two-hour nap. When have I ever done that in recent history?

The day after Christmas I have a basketball tournament in Overland, which is an hour away. Lucy and Dad have colds and Carson doesn't want to go, so Mom and Eva are the only family in the stands. I keep messing up. Bad passes, missed shots. I only score four points and move like I'm hauling a train around the court.

"Berger. Get the lead out!" Coach keeps yelling.

Eva comes over and hangs on me after we win 47-38. Mom examines my face. "Are you feeling okay?"

"Mmm. Fine." *World's biggest lie.*

She touches my forehead. "You're warm."

"Mom, I'm playing basketball. I get warm."

We have lunch and an hour break before the next game. I lay down on the locker room floor to rest.

"Berger. Get up!" It sounds like the voice is coming through a long tunnel. Someone shakes me awake.

By the time I manage to pry my eyes open, I see half the team staring down at me. Coach helps me sit up. My head throbs and my throat is on fire.

"It doesn't look like Berger's going to be playing the next game," Coach announces.

What?

"Tim, go and tell his mom to meet him at the main entrance in five minutes. Jordan, help him get his stuff together."

He turns to me with a sympathetic smile. "You're burning up kid. Looks like you're coming down with something. Best you don't expose the whole team to it."

CHAPTER 38

"What's mononucleosis?"

"Mono is a virus spread through tears and saliva. You may have picked it up by sharing someone's drink or fork," explains Dr. Hillman.

My mind flashes back to the winter dance—to Monica and me sharing a drink.

"Stress can play a part," Dr. Hillman continues. "When someone's immune system is weak it's easier to get sick. Anyway, this explains why you've been so tired the last few weeks, Rourke."

"Will he need medicine?" Mom asks.

"No, just a lot of rest. He's lucky to be on winter break so he won't miss school. If he's feeling better, he can go back after break is over."

"What about basketball?"

Please don't say I need to miss basketball!

"I checked your spleen and it isn't enlarged. If it was, you'd be out for four weeks. I suggest you don't play for ten days, then come back and see me to be sure everything's okay."

I nod with relief. Ten days will be January fifth. We don't have any games until the eighth.

I sleep most of my vacation. No bad dreams and no Carson break-ins. Only reassurance from Sam.

On New Year's Eve, my parents have friends over. Mom comes to say goodnight and hands me a letter. There's no return address, but I recognize the writing.

Dear Rourke (aka Fred),

How's your Christmas break? Dad brought the cookies home Sunday and they were yummy! I liked the gingerbread ones with the white frosting and red-hot candies for buttons. Thank you for bringing them. Did you decorate them? Mom and I used to do that with my sister.

Dad and I drove to Chicago to see my sister, Avery, over Christmas. She's nine and lives with my aunt. She wants me to live with her but Dad wants me with him.

I go to the shelter soon to volunteer. Dad doesn't want me to go but they give me a meal and it's important to help others.

I made this for you. It's a knothole that fell out of a board in the old barn.

Happy New Year from your Girl Scout

P.S. Please don't tell anyone I live in a trailer because the county might make me go to a foster home if they find out.

My Girl Scout? And Grace has a sister? I guess there's still more to learn about this girl.

Maybe it's the mono on top of the holidays making me all mushy, but my eyes get a little wet.

I look in the envelope and shake her gift onto my bed. The wooden knot has a little hole with a piece of twine through it making it into a necklace. I study the wooden knot and rub it between my fingers. It's so smooth. I wonder if the knot in my stomach could ever be smoothed out.

I re-read the letter. I don't get it. Why does she think the county would send her to a foster home for living in a trailer home?

My eyes find Carson's sign that covers the hole he kicked in my door. Maybe worrying about Carson isn't as bad as being separated from your sister and not having a mom.

BY THE TIME school starts up I'm all better, but I only go half days to satisfy Mom. On the first day, study hall with Mad Marlys is a free-for-all.

Bart, the Self-Anointed Great One, announces, "Berger's got the kissing disease! Girls! Stand back. I know you're dying to kiss him, but you're gonna have to wait a few weeks."

Everyone laughs, of course. I just shake my head and pretend to do my art assignment on perspective drawing. Big-Mouth Bart knows how to get the word out. Someday he'll make it big in the advertising industry.

"Maybe he got it from me!" yells Rudy. The entire study hall erupts.

Before Mom picks me up at noon, I push a note through the narrow vent on Grace's locker.

Dear Girl Scout,

Thanks for the letter and wooden necklace. It's cool. I hung it on the corner post of my bed. Rubbing it relaxes me. Maybe you could go into business making millions more. Your business could be called Girl Scout Designs or something. Then you'd be rich and could build a mansion for your family.

I have mono, which means I want to sleep all the time.

I don't have a present for you but maybe I can give you a second dance lesson.
Happy New Year,
Fred

After school Mom drives me to Dr. Hillman for my checkup.

"You can resume basketball practice next week, but take it easy. And if you have to kiss a girl, make sure she's a pretty one!"

My face warms as he and Mom have a laugh.

CHAPTER 39

The rain feels like it's coming through my brain.
~Carson

On Wednesday, school is cancelled because we have freezing rain and the superintendent isn't excited about buses sliding into ditches.

Carson runs around in his Superman slippers turning lights on and off. Eva and Lucy dress up in old Halloween costumes. Dad went into work early to supervise salting the sidewalks on campus, and Mom is working from home, which means she'll be on the phone all day. I just overheard her tell someone it's a great time to sell a house. A half hour ago she told someone else it's a great time to buy a house. This explains why she's so successful at her real estate job.

I hang out listening to music, but even that gets old, so I wander into Carson's room. He's on his laptop.

"Spell 'financial.'"

"What?" I ask.

"Spell 'financial.'" He hands me paper and a pencil.

"Why?"

"I need financial stickers."

"I don't think they make financial stickers." I write the word down anyway.

He searches for "financial stickers" and up pops hundreds of budget-minded stickers.

"See?"

I laugh. "Carson, you're always right."

"I h-h-hate that sound."

"What sound?"

He looks at the window, where the icy pellets are hitting the glass pane. His sensory system is on high alert. "Carson, we get a day off of school, so you should be loving the sound!"

"I hate that sound."

As I leave, I glance out his window. Some nutty kid wearing an oversized red coat shuffles down the street, trying not to slip. He skates up the sidewalk holding his hood in place so it won't blow off and steps off the curb in the direction of the Salzmanns'. Who would be walking to their creepy place on such a bad day? Or ever?

Just like that, the kid's legs go out from underneath him, and he falls hard on his back. His head snaps back and hits the curb. Ouch!

I hurry downstairs and dig around in the hallway closet for my binoculars. I haven't used them since Old Man Salzmann's scary visit. I move to the window and see the person is up but limping. Although I have the binocs trained on the kid, his hood hides his face. The barking dogs bring the old man out. As the person steps onto the porch he turns his head and takes his hand off his hood to point at the howling beasts. The strong wind blows his hood off. I adjust the manual focus on my binoculars and gasp.

No way!

Grace yanks her hood back up and turns to enter the house with Mr. Salzmann.

No, don't go inside that house!

I lower my binocs and stare at our neighbor's door. *Why would Grace be going there? Did she walk all the way from her trailer in this bad weather? I'm telling Mom. No, I'll go over there myself.*

With my mind racing, I picture the bruises on Grace's arms and worry she's been to the Salzmanns' before. *She wouldn't go somewhere unless she knew it was safe, would she?* I'd never go over there, and I'm their neighbor!

I run to the freezer and grab a handful of leftover Christmas cookies and stick them in a plastic container. I dig through the wrapping paper cabinet and find a blue bow and tape it to the top of the container. Grabbing my jacket, I bolt out the door and wipe out on the first icy step. Ahh! My elbow hits the concrete but I manage to hold onto the cookies. I penguin-walk the treacherous journey down our sidewalk, into the street, and up the Salzmanns' drive. How in the world did Grace make it all the way from her trailer on this stuff?

This is the first time I've had an up close and personal look at the Salzmanns' mutts. Since they didn't take a bite out of Grace maybe they'll leave me alone too. Naturally, they bark as soon as they smell me. The front door opens. No need for a doorbell, I guess, when you've got attack dogs announcing your presence.

It's Randall, who—according to Dad—was recently discharged from the army. Today it looks like he just rolled out of bed. Unshaven and leaning in a cocky manner against the doorframe in his boxers and GO ARMY shirt, he squints at me like I've just crossed the enemy line.

"Uh, my mom wants me to give you these Christmas cookies." Of course, Christmas was two weeks ago.

Silence.

I lift the cookies toward him. After what seems like an eternity, he reaches out and takes them. Without taking an eye off me, he opens the lid, picks one cookie out, and dramatically bites off Rudolph's red nose.

I take a quick glance past Randall into the house, which looks surprisingly normal with a dog napping on the wood floor.

"Thank your mother," he mumbles as cookie crumbs spray out between his teeth.

I nod and he closes the door, but not before I notice his artificial leg and hear Grace coughing her head off somewhere inside.

IT's AFTER MIDNIGHT. I'm exhausted, and yet I can't sleep. I lift my shade and look at the Salzmann house, praying Grace is okay.

Frost's poem drifts into my thoughts. *Nothing gold can stay.*

I think about all the Ponyboys and Graces and Carsons of the world. I picture their challenges and bleak futures stacked on top of each other and shiver as hopelessness worms in.

I drift in and out. Finally, I sit up on the edge of my bed with my pillow in my hand and move to the hall. Maybe I can sleep better on Mom's white sofa. When I get to the hall, I stop and watch my spooky shadow thrown against the wall from the nightlight.

I turn and shuffle into Carson's room. Standing over him with my pillow hanging in one fist at my side, I take time to study his face. The nightlight allows me to see the rise and fall of his chest. He looks so serene.

My toes run into a line of soldiers and they fall like dominoes. Carson doesn't stir. He's got his earplugs in.

I climb into bed beside him and listen to his breathing. I imagine him as a boy who doesn't flap or bust through doors. He hits homeruns and has a million friends. No one teases him or crushes him with a bus. He grows up to be an astronaut or musician or Superman.

I drift into a wonderful dream. *We're little, maybe four or five years old, and hiding under Carson's bed when Dad comes home from work. Dad hears us giggle and calls out, "Carson! Rourke! Where are those little Berger brothers?" And when Dad finds us, he tickles us until we can hardly breathe.*

I jerk awake and it takes a few seconds for me to figure out where I am. I get up from Carson's bed, careful to not wake him.

"What are you doing, Rourkey?" My body jumps as if I've been prodded with a hot iron. It's Eva.

"Nothin'." I whisper as I bolt from Carson's room. "Just going to the bathroom." She's standing in the hallway clutching her thread-worn blanket. In the dim light she stares at my pillow.

I toss it into my room and walk to the bathroom, not bothering to turn on the light. I'm icy cold so I run hot water into my hands and splash it onto my face and arms.

Back in my own bed, sleep finds me, but so does the mother of all nightmares.

MORNING COMES. My head feels the size of Texas. I'm woozy like I've been on a boat for a month and my mouth is sandpaper dry. Is it the mono? I try to stand, but my legs are wobbly. I sit back down. Eva comes to my door. She spies my pillow on the floor.

Ahhhhh! A speeding bullet hits my chest.

"Carrrrson!" I scream his name like the devil himself is after me. I half run and half crawl down the hallway to his room, screaming his name, tripping on the hallway runner.

My bloodcurdling screams bring the entire family to Carson's room. His body is gone. They've taken him already. I'm on my knees, hands clasped together, shaking my head back and forth. I turn and my parents are staring at me as if they're looking at a madman.

I grab at my father's leg but miss.

"Rourke, what on earth?" Dad's got his arms around the twins, holding them back from me.

"I need to make my bed," someone says. The someone is Carson.

My body stiffens. My throat stops moaning. I twist around and stare at the ghost who just walked into the room.

"You're still here?" I manage to squeak.

Carson stares at me and repeats his demand. "I need to make my bed. And fix my army guys."

Dad helps me up from the floor and sits me on Carson's bed. Mom feels my forehead.

"Rourke, what's the matter? Were you having a nightmare or something?"

I collapse against Dad's shoulder in relief. "Yes, a horrible nightmare."

"I need to make my bed." Carson repeats. The sweetest six words I've heard in my life. For once, I can't wait to hear him say it again. I reach out and touch Carson to be sure he's really there. He pulls away.

Mom looks at me with concern. "You don't look well, honey."

You wouldn't look well either if you had a nightmare about someone hurting your brother.

CHAPTER 40

"It was nice of you to bring cookies to the Salzmanns."

Grace's froggy voice within a foot of my ear startles me, causing me to hit my right elbow on the sharp edge of my locker door. My other elbow is still tender from the fall on the icy steps. Now I have a matching set.

"Grace! Hey! You're okay!" I'm so glad to see her in one piece I forget I'm upset over her trip to the Salzmanns.

In between some pretty harsh coughs, she says, "Of course I'm okay."

Rubbing my elbow, I waste no time digging into what's been eating me the last few days.

"What on earth were you doing at the Salzmanns'?" I didn't mean for it to come out so harsh. I seem to have no filters anymore. Ever since the nightmare, I've been a mess.

She rears back. "I'm not sure why it's any of your business." Her voice matches my tone.

I notice a bandage on her forehead, and she's coughing her lungs up, but I refuse to get distracted.

"Look, I'll tell you why. Those neighbors of ours are scary, like horror picture show scary. And why in the world were you out slip-sliding around in an ice storm?"

"You were spying on me?" She spits out her words.

Sick of this, I yell, "No! I don't even know where you live because you won't tell me so how can I spy on you? I just happened to be looking out my window and happened to see someone *dumb* enough to be out ice skating on the curb."

Kids stop to stare at us. We move to the side of the hall.

"Then how did you know it was me?" she hisses.

"I saw your..." My voice trails off.

"You *were* spying." She has a winning look on her face. *Are girls always this exasperating?*

"Your hood blew off. Where did you get that get-up anyway?"

"If you must know, the jacket belongs to someone at the homeless shelter. They let me borrow it."

"You didn't answer my other question. Why were you at the Salzmanns'? And—" I look at what's left of her hair. "What in the world happened to your hair?"

She presses her lips together tight and crosses her arms over her chest.

"Fine." I raise both hands in defeat, slam my locker door shut, and head to lunch.

She calls after me. "I'm just staying with them a while. Rourke, it's no big deal."

I halt. I turn and walk back to her, moving in so close I feel her breath on me and see the fiery flecks of green raging in her brown eyes.

I spit my answer in her face. "Yes, Grace. This is kind of a big deal. And here's why. Those Salzmanns are all men. Big men. You're a girl. They're not the type who sit around the campfire singing Kumbaya. They have guns and monster mutts. And you're *living* with them?"

She stands her ground, her chin up in the air. "And just why do you care?" Each word jabs me a little more than is comfortable.

My eyes bulge wide and through clenched teeth I bark, "I *don't* care."

Regretting my comment immediately, I grab her wrists. She flinches and moans in pain. I push up the long baggy sleeves covering her hands. "You already have Daddy or Old Man Salzmann or someone hurting you."

I look down to expose her bruised forearms but instead I see one arm and hand is bandaged and the other arm has a nasty burn blister.

Grace tries pulling her arms away, but I'm so shocked that I hang on.

"Who's doing this to you?"

Her eyes swell with tears as she struggles to break my grip. I let go and Grace stumbles backward, nearly falling. She turns and runs into the girl's bathroom, coughing herself to pieces.

I sense Sam's presence and can tell he's shook. The group of students that stopped to stare moves on. Across the hall, Miss Thompson stands in her doorway.

Sam suggests I go home to cool off, so I drag myself to the school nurse. Mom picks me up, and I sleep all day.

CHAPTER 41

*Rourke has plenty on his mind without knowing the truth
about me.*
~Grace

Grace hasn't been in school for three days. To get my mind off her, I thumb through my poetry journal while Nicotine Nancy makes an announcement. "The *Hazard Herald* is holding a poetry contest. I sent in a poem from each student journal. The winning poem will be printed in the paper."

Monica calls out, "Cool! I hope I win!"

Nicotine Nancy's expression indicates she doubts it.

Monica is a smart girl but her writing stinks. During share time we exchange journals and read each other's poems. Monica's are always about the mall or winning the lottery, like this one. (Okay, she isn't bad at rhyming.)

Mirror Mirror in the Mall
Who's the fairest of them all?
Is it the suede Gucci bag
With the thousand dollar tag?
Or the leopard Jimmy Choo shoes
That will match my new hairdo?
ATM ATM in the Bank
Who is the richest one I should thank?
Is it my mommy with her rich mommy?

Or is it my daddy with his rich daddy?

I'll save it for our twenty-five-year class reunion so we have something to chuckle about. Of course, by then, Monica will no doubt be a millionaire clothes designer and married to Bart. Ever since the school dance, she's been back with Bart. I guess I was just a stand-in after all.

My mind shifts to Grace and where she'll be in twenty-five years. Shoot, I don't even know where she is now.

"Where are you going?" Mom asks.

"Just biking to Phinney's to get help with my science lab report."

"Honey, I'll drive you. You're just getting over mono."

"Nah, I'm fine."

"Well, take the phone with you then. And don't forget your helmet."

I leave Sam at home. I need to do this alone. I'm depending more and more on him and it's not right.

I ride east to the water tower and head down a side path toward the landfill. The ruts and snow make the going rough, so I get off my bike, leave it under a bush, and walk the direction Grace headed the day we left the old barn.

I pass the junkyard and smell the landfill before I see it. Even though it's winter, the stench makes me gag so I try to breathe through my mouth. Perched on top of a little hill, I look out onto the mounds of trash. I check the other direction for trailers. Nada.

To the left of the landfill is a small woodsy area. The trees barely camouflage a junky horse trailer covered with a tarp.

I don't know why Grace was headed here, but there's no

sign of a mobile home. As far as I know, the trailer homes are all in Northwood Court on the other end of town.

As I make my way back to my bike a clanking sound interrupts the quiet. I glance back and notice two people beside the horse trailer. I move in closer. It's Grace and her dad! I duck down and peer through the bushes. Grace had said they lived "wherever they will let us park our trailer," but she never said it was a horse trailer!

I hop on my bike and ride to Phinney's and spill everything.

Phinney looks at me and sighs. "Maybe it's a lifestyle choice to live the way they do. Some people don't want others in their lives so they go live in the mountains. Grace's dad chose the landfill."

"Phinney, you can't tell anyone. I don't want Grace to get in trouble."

"Scout's honor."

"Thanks."

"But Rourke."

"What?"

"You don't have to figure out everyone's problems, you know."

CHAPTER 42

Growing up is hard.
~Rourke

I write a note to Grace and drop it on her desk as I enter math class.

Dear Grace,

Sorry about the blow up. I was just so shocked to see you at the Salzmanns'. I can't believe you're staying there. Are you related to them or something? I can't sleep because I worry they might hurt you.

When Carson gets into some predicament, I don't want people asking me about it but I guess they're trying to help. I have someone who helps me understand Carson. Sometime maybe I'll tell you about him. Do you have someone helping you?

Rourke

P.S. What happened to your face and arms and hair? Also, my grandma always said tea with honey helps a cough.

Before Social Studies I see a note stuck in my locker.

So you do care.

Meet me at the old barn at 10:00 Saturday. GS

Grace is right. I do care. I like being around her. She's smart and full of surprises. All I can think of is our last conversation by my locker, seeing her injured arms, her chopped hair, and accusing her of things she may have no control over.

Sam warns me about the risk of meeting Grace Saturday, but I do it anyway. At the water tower I slow my bike and consider turning back. I take in a big breath and continue to the barn. The door is open just enough to give me a glimpse of Grace doing some target practice with the wimpy bow.

I'm a little jumpy. If I confront her about seeing her at the trailer she'll accuse me of spying again.

"Hi." My voice sounds as flat as Carson's. Grace turns but doesn't say a thing. I look at her and wonder who the real Grace is. Are her stories about her family all made up, like my Sam? I already have Carson to worry about. The last thing I need is someone else to lose sleep over.

Grace comes over to pull the door back enough to get my bike inside. I stand with my hands in my coat pockets. I want to look at her. I always want to look at her. But I don't. Is this the way Carson feels all the time? Anxious about looking at people because he's afraid of what they'll think or say?

She starts right in. "I'm not related to the Salzmanns."

I steal a look at her. She's got a knitted hat pulled over most of her chopped hair and, with the exception of her red eyes, she still looks great to me.

"They take in homeless people." She registers my disbelief and nods. "Yeah. They're so nice."

Nice wouldn't be the word I'd use to describe my strange neighbors, but it's best I don't say it.

"Dad and I are homeless. Well, we had the trailer, but it wasn't much of a home."

"I know." My confession comes out easily.

"You know what?"

I swallow hard but hold her stare. "You had all those bandages on at school and then you weren't in school for a while…"

She leans her head back and looks ready to bust.

She won't like this part.

"You walked toward the landfill after the first time we met here so I-I—"

"You spied on me."

Biting my lip, I try to nod but my head decides it doesn't want to move. I'm caught in her stare.

"Well, it was just a place to sleep." She turns away and continues as if my discovery doesn't matter.

"My dad—he works most of the time, and I'm in school or volunteering so we weren't in the trailer much anyway." She sits, using a bale as a backrest. Her words spill out faster. "But it's been so cold, so we had to use more than one space heater. That's what caused it."

Caused what? Have I caught the beginning and end of some mystery movie but dozed off in the middle?

"The day we didn't have school…because of the ice storm? Dad wouldn't let me stay in the trailer. He said I'd freeze to death. The libraries and churches were all closed. It wasn't my day to volunteer at the shelter so I had nowhere to go, and they don't like me hanging around at Dad's work."

"Why can't you guys just stay at the homeless shelter? Isn't that what it's for?"

"Dad doesn't want anyone to know about our situation. In fact, you're the only one I've told. He's afraid they'll separate us and force me into a foster home if the social workers get involved. That would kill him."

"So he thinks our scary neighbors are better than the shelter? Does he have a clue what kind of people they–" I'm getting loud but she cuts me off.

"The lady in charge of the homeless shelter told me about them, and Dad checked them out. They help all kinds of people. Disabled people, war vets who can't find jobs or need an arm or a leg. People just down on their luck."

Someone needs an arm or a leg? What is she talking about?

"Mr. Salzmann's wife and daughter were killed last year by a drunk driver. He got a bunch of money from a lawsuit plus insurance money and is making a memorial in his backyard in honor of his daughter."

Which explains the hunk of wood and late-night chainsaw noise.

"He used some of the money for his own rehab, but the rest he's using to help people who need a break. And Randall is using some of the money to research ways to disarm IEDs."

"IEDs?"

"Improvised explosive devices. Randall served in Afghanistan. His job was to disable roadside bombs. One exploded and ripped off his leg. He's had a dozen surgeries, and now he's working on ways they can use drones instead of people to disarm hidden bombs."

In that old camper on our street? How can my family live right beside them and not know any of this?

"He and his buddy who lost both legs just landed a grant to work on it."

"But you're living there? I thought you said your dad won't accept a handout."

"He cut a deal with Mr. Salzmann and is fixing a vehicle for him."

I repeat myself, only louder. "So you're gonna live with them?" I still am not buying this.

"Well, that wasn't the plan," she replies. "The day after the ice storm I walked back to the trailer so I could change clothes and go to school. Dad was at work." Her words fade away.

She takes a deep breath and rubs her bandaged hand.

Don't tell me anything more. Please, no more.

"It was so cold." Her voice is a whisper. "Our gas space heaters had been off for a while since no one was there, so I turned them both on. But it wasn't enough. So I turned on the gas hot plate, too." The color has drained from her face.

"Stop!" I shake my head back and forth as tears sting my eyes. A cramp slices through my gut. She doesn't stop.

"It was my fault. Somehow my sleeves caught fire when I reached across to turn it down. When I tried getting the sweater off, my hair caught on fire."

Her beautiful hair.

"I rolled in the snow to get it out and then walked to the station. Dad borrowed his friend's car and brought me to the emergency room." She is out of steam, and I have no words.

I glance at the bandage on her forehead.

Reading my mind, she reaches up and touches it. "I hit my head on the metal doorframe when I was trying to get out of the trailer in a hurry. Just a few stitches."

I sit beside Grace and put my hand on her bandaged one. She leans her head on my shoulder. After a minute I get the courage to ask her the dreaded question.

"Those bruises on your arms. Is someone hurting you?"

"No. Well, kind of."

I don't want to hear this part.

"There was this crazy guy at the shelter. I wasn't the only one. He would grab people and not let them go. He wasn't trying to hurt us but he had some mental problems... He's not there anymore."

"And the cuts and scratches on your wrists and hands? You're not trying to hurt yourself?"

She looks shocked at my suspicions. "I would never do that. No, those were from digging through bushes and wire fences to find the rabbits I shot with my bow. One time my knife slipped when I was skinning a rabbit and I accidentally cut myself." She points to her scar.

She can tell I'm having a hard time absorbing all this. "We would make stew with the rabbits. You know—to eat."

She holds my gaze, and I have no choice but to believe her. "So you wear long baggy sleeves to cover them up."

She exhales and smiles her million-dollar smile. "Yes, and now I'm your neighbor."

After a long silence, I find my voice again. "You did a lousy job cutting your hair." She laughs and groans at the same time.

CHAPTER 43

All my Superman shirts are in the washer. Now what am I going to wear?
~Carson

Well, if Grace was my neighbor, she's not anymore. I went to the Salzmanns' after basketball practice. I figure if Grace isn't afraid of them, why should I be? Peter came to the door.

"Moved out yesterday. For privacy, I can't discuss guests." He says it like he's a hotel manager.

As I turn to leave, Peter says, "Tell Carson hi for me."

"Uh—sure."

"You're lucky," he says.

For a few seconds, our eyes lock.

"Why's that?"

"You have Carson."

No one has ever told me that before.

"And you have sisters. And a mother."

My stomach tightens. There's pain in his eyes. I nod and walk home where Mom is folding laundry. "Homework today?" she asks.

"Yep, I'm going to get started now."

Instead of doing homework I sit at my desk thinking about Peter and his loss. Sam tells me I better not start worrying about Peter now too.

I pull out some paper and start writing.

Grace,
What happened so you guys have to live in a horse trailer?
If you don't want to tell me, it's okay. And where are you now?
Peter told me you left.
Rourke

I stuck the note through the vent slots in Grace's locker two days ago, but she hasn't been in school. I rode my bike to her trailer twice, but it's empty.

Today she comes to school with icicles hanging from her hair.

I lean against the locker next to Grace's and wait for the answer to my silent "What now?" question.

"It's not very warm in a tent."

She's upgraded to a tent?

During math I stare at the back of her head. The icicles are gone but her uneven haircut reminds me of the fire, and by lunchtime I can't stand it. "I need to talk to you."

We sit together at lunch for the first time, but neither of us eats the overdone burgers on our tray. "What happened? I mean, why are you living in a horse trailer?"

"My mom died of cancer. My parents thought they had good insurance, but not for cancer, I guess."

"So your dad spent all his money on your mom." That didn't come out right.

"Dad sold our house, cars, furniture, everything to pay her medical bills. And then he lost his job. He just wanted to be with her those last few weeks. But it turned into six months, and Dad's boss couldn't keep paying someone who wasn't in the courtroom every day."

"The courtroom?"

"Dad's a lawyer."

"Couldn't you stay with relatives?"

"We did. With Aunt Belle. But after Mom died and the economy tanked, Dad had trouble finding a job where he wasn't traveling. When his cousin gave him this temporary job fixing cars, Avery stayed with Aunt Belle, and I moved here with Dad."

I tap on my lunch tray with a fork. "You're living in a tent now?"

"We're freezing in the tent." Her eyes fill with tears. "Dad says we need to go to the homeless shelter tonight."

We throw away our cold food.

I write a note to Grace during science and stuff it in her locker.

Grace, I'm so sorry about your mom. That really sucks. I don't know what I'd do if one of my parents died. I bet your mom was amazing and that you are like her. Because you are amazing.

You and your dad can live with us. I know my parents would be fine with it. And Carson would love it.

Rourke

CHAPTER 44

I have friends. Some of them are things.
~Carson

I make a pledge to myself to not let anything bother me today because it's game day. We play our archrival, Allentown, and the team is pumped! I have a great feeling about this game because my energy is totally back. Plus, if we win, Bart's having a party Saturday night. In his usual manner of inviting he told me, "Berger, be there or find yourself a different lunch table next week."

I slide onto the kitchen bench beside Carson and grab a banana from the fruit bowl.

"Good morning, Carson!" He already has his backpack on. "Man, what's in your backpack anyway? It's sagging a bit! Could it be your key collection?"

A wide smile lights up his face. "And my stickers and my numbering journal."

Mom smiles at me. "Someone's in a good morning mood for a change."

"Sure am. It's game day, Mom!"

Mom laughs. "So this is what it takes to make Rourke Berger happy at seven-thirty a.m.—a basketball game?"

"Yep, and a couple other things," I say.

"Well, I'd like to hear what those are, but we're running low on time. Carson, you better get those teeth brushed before you head out."

Carson grumbles and shuffles up the steps.

"Mom, shouldn't Carson walk with his own friends to school pretty soon?"

"In an ideal world, yes," said Mom, "but I don't think Carson has friends to help him out. Right now, you go to the same school and your father and I need to get the girls to their school and ourselves to work on time. We need you to help with Carson. Which reminds me. You're babysitting for the girls and Carson the night of my big Starlight Gala. This year we're expecting to raise enough money to build another home for a low-income family! Dad and I are counting on you."

She smiles that mom smile that leaves me with no suitable comeback.

"No problem, Mom. Come on, Carson, or we'll be late."

"No!" Carson barks as he comes down the stairs. "I-I-I-I'm not late. I can never be late for school."

Sam gives me his *stay calm* look.

I tap my fingers on the counter as I turn toward Carson who still has his Superman slippers on. I try a different tactic. "If you hurry we can count all the cool cars on the way."

Carson looks at his feet, pondering my idea. His face transitions to "all right then," and he puts his shoes on faster than I've ever seen him do it. "Let's go, Rourke. Y-y-y-you're going to be late."

This cracks me up.

"Goodbye, boys!" Mom calls. "Good luck at your game, Rourke. We'll be there to cheer you on."

We count fifty-eight cars on the way to school.

As I walk into school, there are all kinds of signs the cheerleaders put up on the walls and lockers to advertise the game.

I hustle to homeroom in time for the morning announcements. The principal goes through the usual: lunch menu, after school activities—including our game with Allentown—and a reward for anyone who knows the responsible party who plugged the boys' toilet again.

"One last announcement today. The winner of the seventh-grade *Hazard Herald* poetry contest is—Rourke Berger! Congratulations, Rourke! Look for his poem in the Herald!"

Wow! I'm curious which of my poems Nicotine Nancy submitted for the competition.

The day flies by. When science ends, Miss Thompson wishes me good luck as I head out the door.

"What are you, the teacher's pet?" It's Bart. "She didn't wish me good luck."

"Maybe it's because I need luck and you don't, Bart."

"Ahh...yes. I have talent on my side."

And modesty.

As I hurry to the locker room after school, I round the corner by the cafeteria and collide with a girl. In an effort to keep upright I grab her shoulders and hold on. "Whoa! I'm sorr—"

"Rourke, it's you!"

It takes me but a second to realize I have my arms around Grace.

"Hi. Hey, I'm sorry. I'm hurrying so I'm not late for the big game."

Grace giggles. "Okay, then hurry! I hope you win!"

Running backwards, I say, "Yep! Wish you could make the game." I want to say more, like "I wish you had a mom and a house and someone to give you a better haircut."

She waves, and I run off silently cheering with Sam at my side.

The Allentown Tigers come out of the girls' locker room

with bright orange jerseys that look like they just came from the factory. A roaring tiger outlined in black is on the front of them. We are the Hazard Hornets, and although our uniforms aren't new, they look sharp too with a big gold hornet on black.

"Go eleven!" It's Dad's voice, and man it's good to have him at my game!

I hear Carson too. "Go eleven. C'mon, Rourke. Go eleven. Go eleven. Go eleven."

Coach Piper meets with us in the locker room before the game starts. "Boys, we want to look sharp in front of our fans. How many have families here today?" Every boy raises his hand except Bart who is fiddling with his shoe ties.

"Great! It's important to have family support. Now here's the starting lineup. Justin Overby and Bart Hurtle as forwards, Jordan Green and Rourke Berger as guards, and Too Tall Tim Lyons as center."

All right! My first start! I keep my gaze trained on the coach to avoid Adam Johnson's eyes. I've taken his starting spot.

We head into the gym as the starters are announced and the cheerleaders cartwheel across the floor. I exchange looks with Phinney who is seated in the student section. I'm not sure if he's here to watch me or to see Maggie cheer.

For the first half of the game we are in control with a six or seven point lead. I hold my own and am in and out of the game, sharing time with Adam. I make one jump shot from my sweet spot to the left of the free throw line and just miss a three-pointer that rims out.

Too Tall Tim does a great job rebounding and follows up on shots missed. Bart has been called for traveling twice, so Coach pulls him. He stomps off the floor and refuses the towel handed to him.

At half time, Coach tells us we need to be getting more shots off. "You can't score if you don't shoot!"

During the second half, the Tigers gain momentum and the score is soon tied at twenty-nine. The coaches of both teams spend the third quarter off the bench, yelling at players to do this, do that, and slowly we pull away with a nice lead.

Allentown has a player they call Bear; I guess it's because of his woolly hair. He's their sharpshooter and pours it on in the fourth quarter. Pumping in three shots in a row, he puts Allentown ahead, 44-40.

A sure win is slipping away. Bart is wearing down. He's been playing most of the game so has a reason to be tired, but something is off with him today. Justin, our other forward, has put in ten points, but now he reaches in and thumps Bear on the arm. The ref blasts his whistle for Justin's fourth foul. Coach pulls Justin and subs in Adam for me, and I move to Justin's forward position. I've only played this position a few times during practice.

Bear stands at the free-throw line, dribbles twice, and gracefully arcs the ball into the hoop. All net.

We battle back and forth, and I'm struggling to defend Bear. I haven't made any baskets since subbing for Justin even though I've taken three or four shots. The Tigers widen their lead on us, and with just three minutes remaining in the game we are down by eight.

Justin returns, and I get a breather. Adam sinks a three-pointer. The seconds tick away and I'm back in. Too Tall, Bart, and I shoot our hearts out. But our opponents do the same. Jordan fouls a player the Tigers call Glue—probably because he can't jump more than two inches off the floor—to stop the clock with nine seconds left.

Coach calls "time" and tells us his plan. Bart and I will stand near the centerline during the free throw. Too Tall will get the rebound (assuming Glue misses the shot, which is doubtful) and will throw it to Jordan, who will catapult it to either Bart or me for a breakaway layup to win the game.

Glue makes the first free throw. Now we're down by two. The second one goes up, spins the rim, and whips out to Too Tall.

Seven seconds left. The small crowd is screaming.

Too Tall whips the ball hard, causing Jordan to miss it. It rolls over the centerline and into the waiting hands of Allentown's Bear. Bear dribbles with a look of joy, celebrating with five seconds to go. I charge toward him with all I have and steal it mid-dribble before he knows it's gone.

Turning, I pump the ball to Bart who takes two dribbles into a perfect layup, tying the game. The ref's whistle screeches. Bart's been fouled, and the shot counts! No time remains on the clock, but Bart gets to take the free throw. When the ball goes through the hoop, the fan noise practically lifts me to the ceiling with excitement!

CHAPTER 45

I wish I had a brother.
~Phinney

This morning when I pick up the *Hazard Herald,* I flip to the sports page. Only high school sports are covered, so there's nothing about our great win over Allentown. But it doesn't matter, because I already got the best response after the game from Phinney.

He ran onto the court and hoisted me off my feet. "Your steal was something out of the NBA highlights, Rourke!"

As I fold the paper, my school picture on the lower right corner of the front page catches my eye. *Poetry Winner Chosen by Herald.* When you live in a small town I guess this is news. I turn the page to my poem. I vaguely remember writing it. Nicotine Nancy had given us an assignment to write a poem about how differences enrich our lives. I remember thinking about the differences between Bart and Phinney, Monica and Grace, Carson and me.

No Divide
World, your gifts aren't usually a surprise.
Your sunrise golden greets me each morning;
What amazing blues paint your skies;
Night stars count both my yearnings and
   blessings.

Wait! What is this small secret door?
Can I open it? Go inside?
Ah! It's like a music store!
Full of differences with no divide.

Loud and soft, moody and bright;
Everyone treasured in their own special way.
For there's no better or worse—just right.
Overflowing with differences and that's okay.

I set the paper on the kitchen table, staring at the words I wrote. No better or worse—just right. Sam nudges me. *Yes, I know. I need to stop judging people for what I see on the surface.*

And today, I have happier things to think about as Bart's girl-boy party is tonight! I need to tell Mom and Dad about it, but I'm not sure they'll be okay with the girl-boy part.

Mom floats into the kitchen humming "Sweet Caroline" and twirls. She holds two dresses against her body and extends her right arm as if she's dancing with a partner. She sings a couple lines.

"Which dress should I wear to the gala this year, Rourke?"

I point to the pinkish dress with white flowers all over it. It looks more like a gala dress than the black one, which she wore to Grandma's funeral.

"You're right! It's more perky."

Mom sure looks happy. Now might be a splendid time to tell her about the party. "Mom, you deserve a new dress! Why don't you go out and buy a new one?" I try to not sound like I'm up to something.

She laughs. "Rourke, I'd love to! But I don't have time to go shopping before the big event tonight."

Wait! Her gala is tonight?

CHAPTER 46

There are too many rules.
~Carson

"You haven't forgotten about babysitting, have you?" she asks as my stomach drops.

"No, no. I'll be here."

It's useless to even mention the party. I'm stuck here. Mom co-chairs this enormous fundraiser, Stargaze or Starlight event every year. *How did I forget?*

"The girls checked out two movies from the library today. They can watch one and then need to be in bed by eight-thirty. Carson should like the movies they picked out."

In the middle of my pity party, I get a great idea, but Sam warns, *Don't you dare! There will be other parties.*

By seven, Mom and Dad are ready to leave.

"We'll be back before midnight. No need to wait up for us."

I give her a thumbs up.

"Say, Rourke?" I recognize this tone. She's going to ask me to do one more favor. Like, will I sign in blood to take care of Carson for the rest of my life? *I wish I could, Mom. I really do. Just tell me how.*

"Don't forget to sort the laundry and empty the dishwasher tonight. And have you picked up your room this week? It looks like a tornado went through."

"No problem, Mom."

The party starts at eight. I call and tell Bart I'll be late. Sam is stomping around in my head, furious with my decision.

Lucy and Eva sit on the couch to watch a documentary about some scientist who claims he discovered animals once thought to be extinct. Carson lays out a bunch of keys on the carpet end to end. Hank is snoring on Dad's favorite chair, and Beulah is eyeing Carson's keys.

"Make us some popcorn," Lucy insists.

Listening to Lucy's demands and watching Carson sort his keys, I tap my fingers on the counter and eye the time. I should be on my way to Bart's.

When I hear Beulah choking on one of the keys, I yell, "Carson, pick up those keys or I'll chuck them out the window."

"You c-c-c-can't."

"Oh yeah?" I pick up a handful of keys, go to the front door, and toss them in the snow.

Seeing the terror in Carson's eyes, I realize my mistake. "My keys! My keys! They are my favorites."

"You've got a couple hundred other keys, Carson."

"G-g-get my keys! I need them." His voice shakes.

As he runs to his room and locks his door, I slap my head. *Why did I do that?*

I go out and dig around in the snow. I don't know if I have them all, but I bring the wet keys in and push them under Carson's door.

"Sorry, Carson."

"Th-Th-Thank you, Rourke."

"Carson?" He doesn't respond.

"Your friend Peter says hi."

"Peter. Peter says hi. My friend Peter says hi."

I can hear him repeating it as I walk downstairs and sit on the sofa between my sisters who snuggle into me. I look at Eva, then Lucy. I have two sisters and a brother. Peter Salzmann's right. I am lucky.

As the twins watch the movie, I close my eyes and listen to Sam. He reminds me of what I already know. Carson likes his collections. Order. Routine. Sam repeats the words of my own poem: *Overflowing with differences and that's okay.*

"Time for bed!" I announce when the movie ends. Eva wants to know why I changed into my church shirt and why I smell funny. Why do sisters never seem to notice anything until you don't want them to?

"You didn't make us popcorn."

"Lucy, it's too late."

"Read us a book."

So I do, and by nine o'clock they're asleep. I go through Carson's schedule with him. "Stay upstairs and count whatever you want and then go to bed when the timer goes off. Don't answer the phone, don't call anyone, and don't answer the door."

"Make me popcorn."

"You know how to make it."

Maybe it will work. Go to the party, leave early, get back before my parents do.

Sam disagrees.

I let both dogs out to pee and grab Mom's cell from the counter.

As I close the garage door, I notice Mr. Salzmann standing by his fence, staring at me. "Where are you going this time of night?" He sounds suspicious.

"Just out for a short ride." I don't care what Grace says, he's scary.

"Where are your sisters?" Creepy question.

"At a sleepover." I'm not about to let him know they're home alone with Carson.

I spend the ten-minute bike ride calculating what time I'll

have to leave the party in order to be home before Mom and Dad return. Ten-thirty should work.

It's January, and no one in his right mind bikes at night in this cold. The temp is above freezing, but the wind bites as I ride.

It's weird that I want to go to a party at Bart's house. I know it's because all my friends will be there and I want to be part of it. But my gut is reminding me of what Sam has been telling me all evening. This might not be my smartest move.

Loud music from a block away leads me to Bart's house. He said to use the back entrance. Phinney and Cockroach are the first ones I see. Phinney gives me a salute. Maggie is holding Phinney's hand. Phinney would never be invited to Bart's party except Maggie is one of Amalia's friends and Amalia is Monica's best friend and of course Monica is here.

Bart is across the room dancing with Hannah Holliday, or Hungry Hannah as most of us call her. She's always eating and always hunting for a boyfriend. Bart waves and announces my arrival. "Rourke Berger is in the house, ladies and gentlemen!"

Heat crawls up my face. I guess it's fashionable to be late.

Phinney strolls over. "Glad you could make it, Rourke-man!" he motions me to the other side of the room where some guys are sprawled on a green sofa. They're reminiscing about the glorious win and sipping sodas.

Family photos line a shelf. Bart, his older druggie brother, his mom. Not a single one with a dad in it.

"Great party, huh?" It's Monica.

"Sure is."

"Want something to drink?"

"Yeah, thanks."

At the soda and popcorn table, she has more questions. "What took you so long to get here?"

"I was doing some weight lifting."

I'm not about to tell her it's because my parents don't know I'm here, and I'm supposed to be babysitting. That I better be back before they return or I'm grounded for life.

A handful of girls are next to us pretending not to listen.

"Let's dance," Monica insists.

"Um," I glance around, looking for Bart.

"We broke up."

"Bummer."

"Not really. Let's go!" She pulls me toward the dancing couples before I have a chance to think how Bart will get back at me, even if she is his ex.

She dances like she was born to do this, and I try to forget about Bart. After all, Phinney thinks I shouldn't worry so much about other people.

"I'm thirsty!" Monica shouts after a couple of songs, so we head to the drinks again. Two girls cling to Monica and lean in to whisper. They look sideways at me and giggle. Okay, I guess this is what goes on at a girl-boy party.

I glance at my watch. I'm shocked Sam hasn't been yelling at me to go home. I could call to check on Carson, but I don't want to wake him.

"Come on!" Monica pulls me back to dancing.

During the next break, I pull my cell phone out and see a bunch of missed calls from home. So much for telling Carson not to call.

As I look at the call list, I get a terrifying thought. Maybe Mom and Dad got home early and they've been calling. Holding my breath, I listen to the first message.

"I'm scared. When are you coming home? I'm s-s-s-scared."

My shoulders relax. Sure enough, it's Carson. I listen to the second message. "I'm gonna make popcorn now."

Then my phone vibrates. What if this one is from Mom or Dad? I swallow and walk toward the doorway, wondering what excuse I could come up with that would warrant leaving my babysitting duties.

I coax my voice to sound normal. "Hello."

"Rourke!"

Whew! It's just Carson again. But...he's on fire.

CHAPTER 47

"Rourke! Fire!"

The room sways.

"O-o-on me! I'm on, I'm on fire! Popcorn burned. House b-b-burning."

Fear floods my body. "Get out!" I scream at Carson.

Carson is sobbing. It's hard to understand him.

"Can't get upstairs. The-the smoke..." He's coughing. Smoke. He said smoke. Smoke kills. *My sisters!*

"Carson! Get out of the house and take Eva and Lucy with you!" My vocal cords have reached their limit.

"My k-keys. My s-s-sticker collection. They... They'll get burned up." His crying is more like that of a wounded animal.

I will my desperation through the phone. "Leave it all. Get out, Carson. Get everyone out *now*!" I pound each word.

The music has stopped. Unaware of anyone in the room, I bolt for the door. As I tear it open, I lose my grip on the phone and it clatters to the floor. My shirt cuff catches on the storm door handle but the ripping doesn't register. Nor does the bloody gash on my forearm caused by the sharp door edge.

Lifting my bike upright, I race alongside it, place my left foot on the pedal and leap onto the seat, already in flight mode.

It's cold out here. My coat is back at Bart's house. And something burns in my left arm.

Carson exaggerates. Maybe the popcorn just got burned in the microwave. For a second I relax and realize I'm prone to overreact.

I should never have told Carson he could make popcorn. I should have done it. He always burns it. I'll have some explaining to do to my friends on Monday morning for leaving the party. Maybe I should go back and explain. I slow my bike.

Then I hear something other than my heart pounding in my chest. A police siren followed by the distinct and air-piercing sound of a fire truck horn. My body stiffens and my heart wants to leave my chest as I hear the sirens get closer.

Somebody called 9-1-1.

I taught Carson how to do it a couple of years ago. Mom was furious at me because he kept "practicing," which meant the police were at our front door more than once.

Two blocks over, numerous vehicles with flashing lights scream down Emerson Street.

Oh no! Horrifying visions of my little sisters trapped in the smoke form in my head. *No. Don't think that way.*

I turn forward again and careen into the curb to my right. I over correct to avoid jamming into it and lose control. The bike leans and tilts left, putting me at a freakish angle to the ground. As the back tire spins around to the front, the bike separates from me. My left hip meets the pavement. I don't even wait for the skid to stop. I push myself off the pavement and will my feet to follow the sound of metal hitting the street. I hop on and continue my flight down Poe Street.

All of the streets in this area are named after poets. Strangely, the names of streets and dead poets go through my head, along with Robert Frost's poem.

My left hip is killing me, but I focus on my destination. Did

Carson call 9-1-1? We used to play cops and robbers in the basement. He'd use the play telephone to call the police, and I'd use the toy handcuffs to lock up the robbers, who were either my sisters or their dolls, or both.

My brain is going haywire. *Focus, Rourke.*

I wish I could fly over the treetops and land in my yard and see everything is fine. Just burned popcorn, nothing more. Carson and my sisters would be sound asleep. False alarm.

I don't see the car parked in front of me until it's too late. I brake and swerve. I manage to avoid the back bumper but the side mirror meets my right shoulder, and I land with a thud on the street. The street is slippery and wet and now I am too. The pain in my right shoulder and arm competes with the left hip pain and cut arm. But it's the nausea building in my gut that's the worst.

Shaking, I lift myself off the ground and have trouble getting back on my bike. The handlebars are bent and the seat is missing. I straighten the handlebars as best I can.

Maybe this is one of those nightmares where I keep trying to get somewhere but stuff keeps happening and I can't make it. I'll wake up in my own bed and I'll remember I was at the best party a seventh-grader could ever hope for.

Without a seat I have to stand up and pedal. My legs are on fire. I'm forgetting to breathe. And my shoulder is more numb than painful. Breathe, breathe.

The sirens have stopped but rotating emergency lights flash in the night sky. Maybe the fire is at the Salzmanns'. They're always burning tires in the backyard. Or maybe...maybe Old Man Salzmann set our house on fire to teach me a lesson for spying on him. He saw me leave.

This is taking way too long. Did I make a wrong turn? I've biked these streets hundreds of times. Not at night, but I know this like the back of my hand. No, here is Dickinson

Ave. I'm on track. The fenced-in elementary school is straight ahead.

My left hand is slippery on the bike handle. As I pass under a streetlight I see blood streaming from the forearm gash onto my handgrip. I'm pedaling but nothing is happening. I fall to the right and in the dim streetlight notice my chain has fallen off. It's snowing and the knot in my stomach is pulling so tight it's threatening to slice me in two.

The bike is toast. I leave it and run at full speed. Rather than go way around the school grounds, I climb the fence. Here I am, in my own little action movie. Am I the hero? The bad guy?

The possibility that all of this is real washes over me. Sam! Help, please help me. I gasp between the sobs, wet saltiness in my mouth. Snowflakes and tears blind me. I can't risk running into anything. *Focus.*

I race across the schoolyard and stumble as my knees buckle in the sand of the long-jump pit. I fall, but at least it's a soft landing.

From the Tessings' backyard I see the fire trucks. *They're at our house!* I will my legs to move faster and use my arms to pump harder. My chest is burning as I suck in the icy night air.

The Tessings' garden fence halts my sprint. Something punctures my leg. I reach down and pull a wire from my thigh and continue racing around the garden, away from the cliff and toward the edge of my nightmare. *Wake up, Rourke, please wake up.*

I race around the Tessings' house. No! Flames shoot from the front windows of our house. Emergency vehicles line the street. I rush to a fireman. My lungs burn, and I try speaking but nothing comes out. He grabs my shoulders and I scream from the pain.

"Andy. I've got a kid here in shock. Get him in the ambulance."

I pull away and will my voice to say something. *Sam I need you please! Where are you? I haven't heard you since I left my house.*

"My brother an-and sisters. Get them." Light headedness takes over. *Don't pass out. Do not pass out.*

"Which rooms?" he yells. I am staring in disbelief at the hot flames scorching my face.

He gets in front of me, inches from my face, and tries again. "Where do they sleep?"

I stare into his eyes and see a reflection of the flames. Without looking up, I point to the second story, not knowing if there even is a second floor anymore.

My knees sink to the ground. Something warm and wet is running down the inside of my legs.

There it is again. The edge of the cliff. I grip it so tight my fingers ache.

This Andy guy is on me, dragging me to my feet and trying to lead me toward the ambulance. Adrenaline snaps me back, and I fight his grasp with the last ounce of energy I have. I run to the front doorway where smoke is spewing. Like a giant claw, two firemen haul me back and sit me down hard on the cold ground. Something heavy and warm is wrapped around me.

Two more firemen come out the front door through a billowing cloud of smoke. They're carrying a stretcher. Ice floods my veins and I begin to shake. Ambulance Andy steps in front of me to block what a kid should never have to see. But some morbid part of me needs to, so I shift, and through the smoke I see them pulling a sheet over... someone.

Terror fills my lungs and a sickening moan I don't even recognize as my own worms its way out of my throat.

My body heaves.

Andy squats in front of me shouting something about parents. Everybody seems to be yelling. The noise and chaos and dread drown me.

All I can do is shake my head back and forth. *Sam, come help me.*

Another stretcher and another sheet. *Oh God, no! Please, no.* Unstoppable sickness builds like a tidal wave. I don't want to see who it is. But I need to.

CHAPTER 48

Nothing is fine.
~Rourke

I beat on Andy until he loosens his grip on one of my arms, giving me just enough time to lurch forward before he tackles me again. The stretchers are less than twenty feet away. Breaking free, I scramble on all fours to reach them, but my eyes sting from the smoke and I inhale a cloud of it. Coughing, I pull away from Andy's hold on my ankle and claw forward.

It's dark and bright all at the same time. The glaring and swirling lights of the emergency vehicles cast just enough brightness on the scene to show me something I never ever want to see again. There are no faces on the stretcher. The sheets cover the bodies. Dead bodies. My sisters are dead. I left them alone to burn to death.

Ugliness eats at my insides. And yet I can't look away. Near the top of both stretchers red hair tumbles out from the sheet. Lucy, Eva. I vomit all over Andy.

I'm in the ambulance and someone is checking my blood pressure and wiping my face. I like the coolness. *What happened? Why am I in an ambulance?*

A man leans over me. His face slowly comes into focus. He's bleeding from scratches. Something smells horrible.

"Hey. I'm Andy, an EMT. What's your name?"

His name jolts my memory as I struggle to a sit up. "My

sisters are—" Before I could finish I vomit again, this time on myself.

Spitting out chunks of vomit, I ask, "Where's Sam?"

"Who?"

"My friend, Sam. Where is he? Is he okay?"

"Where is Sam's room? And your sisters' rooms?"

I look at him like he's nuts. Why is he asking about my sisters? Didn't he see them dead on the stretchers?

Andy has me by the shoulders and shakes me. "Ahh!" Pain sears through my neck.

"Hey kid, stick with me. Where are their bedrooms?"

"Upstairs. On that side." I point, but I'm so disoriented in the ambulance that I have no idea where the house is.

"There's no one left upstairs. Only the dogs were up there. Think kid. Where else would they be?"

"The dogs?"

"No! Your family."

I toss my head back and forth. "Mom and Dad aren't here." Saying their names is enough to suck me down a deep dark hole. Moaning I beg, "Don't tell them! Don't tell them!"

Andy drags me out of the ambulance. My hip is killing me. The outside walls of the house are crawling with fire, mostly on the right side. Andy has a tight hold on me to keep me from collapsing. My left arm is wrapped for some reason. The stretchers have been moved. I begin to sob uncontrollably.

"Exactly *who* was in this house tonight?" Andy yells to gain my attention.

My throat burns and I choke on the smoke.

"My brother and..." I can't say it.

"Who else?" He was in my face now.

"My two sisters." My voice cracks and sounds pathetic.

"Where are your parents?"

At the mention of them I drag my fingernails down my face.

They depended on me to take care of everyone. But I left them alone! I beat my head with my fists.

"Kid! Stop it. Hey, stay with me. What's your name? And where are your parents?"

I am not ever going to tell him.

"His name is Rourke Berger, and his parents are at a fundraiser."

It's Mr. Salzmann. The police ask him questions while Andy drags me to the other side of the yard.

My legs aren't working. I collapse forward in a fetal position, close my eyes, and wail. Carson is still in the burning house. He's burning up just like my sisters and it's because I'm a selfish fool. I had to go to a party and this is what I get. Throw me in and let me burn, too.

I think about Carson and Lucy and Eva being trapped and madly looking for me to help them. Was it burned popcorn causing the fire, or wacko Salzmann? Grace doesn't know how evil he is. I bet he burned her trailer, too.

As I rock back and forth, I imagine Carson calling me. "Rourke!" He's pleading.

"H-h-help me, Rourke!" It sounds so real. I can't stand it, so I cover my ears.

Someone rubs my head. I blink a few times. Superman slippers are standing beside me. "D-d-did you find the rest, the-the rest of my keys?"

I don't know if it's the slippers or the keys question that rips me out of my fog and to full attention. "Carson!" I leap up and fall into him with hysterical relief, holding his smudged face in both hands. "You're alive. You're okay."

Andy yanks at Carson and asks him in an accusing tone, "Were you in the house? Where are your sisters?"

"I like the yellow fire trucks. I don't like red ones. Just yellow ones."

"Carson, I'm so sorry. I shouldn't have left you alone. Oh, thank God you're okay."

"D-d-don't cry, Rourkey." He pets my head like I'm a dog. "I was, I was hiding in the bathtub in the basement. I-I-I called 9-1-1 like you showed me."

Andy summons two firemen, and they grill Carson about Lucy and Eva but he just keeps asking them about their yellow trucks. I let my head fall against Carson's chest and cry like a baby.

"Sam's in there." Carson announces this in a casual way. "He showed me the way out."

I clutch at him. "What did you just say?"

"He's in shock," explains Andy.

"No, he's autistic," I tell Andy.

"Hank and Beulah are d-d-dead." Carson's second announcement.

"Ahhhhh...not the poor dogs too." My moaning voice is raspy and dry.

CHAPTER 49

Rourke teaches me important things.
~Carson

"The dogs are over there." A fireman motions toward the stretchers my sisters are on.

Confusion and grief overwhelm me. I take Carson's hand and together we kneel by their stretchers. The scent of burned hair makes me gag. Carson bravely pulls back one sheet. Hank! I pull the other sheet. Beulah. Dogs! Not girls. Red hair like my sisters, but dogs.

A sense of relief mixed with grief over my dead pets and the realization my sisters are still in the house sweeps through me.

"Where have you been, kid?" The stern voice of a police officer is grilling Carson, who looks like he took a shower with his clothes on.

My brain shifts into high alert, and I jump up to face the officer. "This is my brother. He has autism."

The officer gives me a "so what" look.

Frantic, I turn to Carson, who is shivering. "Where are Lucy and Eva?"

"They're in the b-b-basement. I put them in the tub. With water."

Hearing this, a fireman tears inside the front door but returns in seconds to report to the fire chief. "The upstairs floor has caved in, so the door to the basement can't be reached on this level."

"There's a back entrance to the basement!" I cry.

The policeman and several firemen race to the back. Andy and I are on their heels, dragging Carson with us. They try the door but it's locked. One fireman rams it with his shoulder. Nothing.

"It's got a deadbolt."

"You've got to get my sisters out!" I cry.

One firefighter barks. "Get the axe!"

"No time. This side of the roof is gonna go any second."

"I'll shoot the lock!" the officer yells.

"No!" I scream. "Eva and Lucy might be on the other side."

A crushing pressure against my temples causes me to squat down. I can't faint.

"I-I-I've got the key."

We all look at Carson like he's heaven sent. The light from the flames and the flashing fire trucks illuminate his angel face.

Carson pulls out a lanyard with dozens of keys on it. I squeeze my eyes shut in disbelief. It will take forever to try all those keys. Or maybe the right key is with the others I tossed out in the snow.

When I open my eyes, Carson is handing a single key to a fireman like it's no big deal. The fireman rushes to the door and, miraculously, the key unlocks it.

Two firemen disappear inside, and we watch the flames lick the roof with an intensity I've only seen in movies. With a thunderous crash, part of the roof caves and smothers the basement door. The massive cloud of smoke forces us back toward the swing set. A deafening explosion follows and rips the back half of the basement wide open. Sparks rain down on us. There's no way my sisters or those firemen are making it out of there.

"He stayed with me." Carson's voice is expressionless as usual. "Sam stayed with me and helped."

I turn to Carson and get a sense of something powerful.

"Carson, what happened to him? Where's...Sam?"

"He wouldn't get in the tub with us. He probably burned up."

"Noooo!" I dive forward but Andy pulls me back. There's a painful loosening where my arms meet my shoulders and my throat is raw. I give up and sink to the ground, moaning.

Ahhh, Sam.

I crawl inside myself. I need to fix what I messed up. But I can't bring dead people back. I bolt to the front of the house, where Mom and Dad are standing with the police chief. They're home. And they look horrified.

I panic and run toward Dad's Honda sitting in the Salzmann's driveway. The key will be in the ignition. "No one steals a '98 Honda with no air or radio," Dad always says. I jump in and lock the doors.

My hands shake. "Turn the key." I barely recognize my own voice. I squeeze my eyes shut and turn it. *Vroooooom.*

I can't hear much over the roar of the engine, but someone's pounding on the windows, yelling at me. They should step away so they don't get hurt.

I close my eyes to picture Dad's hands and feet and concentrate with every cell of my brain to recall the next step. When I open my eyes, Dad's face is in front of the windshield. "Rourke, get out!"

Reach foot to pedal. I'm too short. I scoot up and push the pedal. A roaring sound, but the car isn't moving. There's so much screaming. My jaw aches from clenching my teeth.

I try the other pedal—no sound. That must be the brake, so I hold my foot on it.

I picture Dad's hands on the shifter and can see him pulling it down when he backs the car out of the garage. I yank it down. Nothing moves. Then I remember my foot on the brake, so I let it go.

The car crashes forward into a trash can, and I hear screaming. My foot hits the brake causing me to slam forward and hit my chin on the steering wheel. This is harder than I thought.

"You'll kill somebody!" someone yells.

Tears fill my eyes and my nose is dripping. I sniff and swipe at my face to clear my vision. My aching fingers grip the wheel. How does a car go backwards? I fiddle with the shifter and ease my foot off the brake. I'm not moving, so I push the gas pedal and the car flies backward. There is some serious yelling, and I hit something—hard. Maybe the mailbox. I crush the brakes and jerk to a stop. My head whiplashes back and then forward into the steering wheel.

Someone is smashing the window with something. There's an explosion by my left ear, and now it's burning. I reach up to touch it and find it wet. Bloody.

I'm in the street. *Now how do I go forward again?* I push the shifter down and the car lurches ahead. Some nuts are beating on the car.

Steer. Turn. Too far. My hands are slippery on the steering wheel. Sweat, or maybe blood. Dad should be working with me on my driving. I turn the wheel back, now the other way. Finally, I'm weaving my way out of the cul-de-sac. We live near the edge of town, and soon I'm headed into blackness.

Relief rushes through me. I made it. But I hear sirens again. *Now what's burning?* I'm drained. I can't go back and face my parents and life without little Lucy and Eva. Exhaustion causes my arms to drop off the wheel, making the car veer to the left before I grab it again.

I drive down the middle of the road because the ditches are

so close. I swear I'm flying, but the dash tells me I'm only going thirty-five mph.

It's hard to concentrate, and the siren sounds like it's in the backseat.

I maneuver the car around a sharp bend, brake haltingly to a stop, and turn off the lights. The car starts to roll when I take my foot off the brake so I move the shifter into park. I get out and crawl to the ditch and sob. I don't even notice I've left the engine running.

"I need somebody!" I gasp at the words and shiver. "Sam!" My weak scream goes unanswered. "Who's gonna help me now?"

The snow has stopped but it's deep in the spot where I'm sitting. My body shivers and my stomach lurches from smoke and self-pity. I notice the stars. They look the way I feel. Far away. Lonely.

I tuck myself into a ball and cover my ears.

The police car rams the back of Dad's car. I watch it slide toward me in slow motion.

CHAPTER 50

This is not heaven.
~Rourke

"Hey! He's waking up!" It's Eva's sweet angel voice. She's on my left side, petting my white wrapped arm.

"It's about time!" Lucy is on my right, poking my other arm.

I get to be in Heaven with my sisters? Someone has granted me more than I deserve. I attempt to sit up, but everything is tight and sore. I thought there was no pain in Heaven. And the lights! *Someone dim them, please.*

"Rourke, honey, we're here. You're fine now. We're all fine." It's Mom. She's crying.

Fine? Heaven is fine? Then why are people crying?

"We're so glad you're okay." It's Dad, and he's crying too.

It takes me all of twenty seconds to realize this is not Heaven. I'm in the hospital.

I bolt upright. A sharp burning pain shoots up my arm.

"Careful, you just pulled your IV out." Mom's face is in front of me but her voice is so far away.

I look around. Carson, Lucy and Eva, Mom, and Dad. But no Sam.

I jerk my head around in desperation and breathe heavy as if I've just been pulled from a shark tank. My eyes dart back and forth. "Where is he?" I push the sheets back and try to get out of bed.

"Take it easy." Dad holds me down.

I attempt to shout but my voice is a weak, pathetic whisper. "Lucy and Eva got out?" I begin to cry in disbelief. "But not..." I sob and rock my head in my hands.

Lucy and Eva crawl up onto my hospital bed, and I hug them with as much strength as I can. Mom and Dad have the three of us wrapped in their arms. Through my tears, I see Carson standing by the window flapping his bandaged hands.

"Why were you in the basement?" I manage to squeak out.

"Carson woke us up to watch another movie," Lucy explained.

"Y-y-you said I c-c-could have popcorn." Carson's voice sounds even. "You told me to p-p-put the microwave on the popcorn setting, but that's not r-r-right. Don't do that, Rourke. When you make popcorn, don't do that. Don't do that."

I went to Bart's party and left them alone.

Dad finishes the story. "Carson said the popcorn bag started on fire in the microwave so he used an oven mitt to grab it but it caught fire too. When he dropped it in the sink, the flames found the curtain. And an oily frying pan in the sink probably didn't help."

"I tried putting it out with water but the fire blew up bad!"

"Water makes an oil fire worse, Carson. You were lucky to only get mild burns." Mom's voice quivers.

"It was too cold to go outside so we filled the basement tub with water and sat in it," said Lucy. "I saw that on TV once." She smiles, all proud of herself.

Carson's arms and hands are wrapped. I reach out my good arm to him. Everyone moves to make room for Carson to sit by me. I lean into him and cry for him, for all of us, and choke out in my most desperate voice, "I'm sorry, Carson. I'm sorry. It's all my fault. I'm so sorry."

When I've cried myself out, I notice Carson clutching his

lanyard that holds dozens of keys. He picks out one from the bunch and holds it between two fingers to show me. "I made the fireman give it back to me."

"If it wasn't for his key, the fire department wouldn't have had a way to get to the girls in time." Dad isn't having much luck trying to get his voice to sound normal either. "When the roof caved in blocking the doors, the firefighters took Eva and Lucy out the basement window."

I stare at the key. Carson's key saved my sisters? The key blurs. My brain is in a fog. I need to sleep.

Phinney comes to visit me. "How's it going, Rourke-man?" His smile is genuine, and he pats me on the head.

"Just another day in paradise."

"Yeah? Paradise sounds scary."

I nod. "A lot of things are scary."

Phinney gives me a long, deep stare. "Rourke. It takes all kinds of kinds, remember? Like in your award-winning poem: Full of differences and that's okay."

I turn toward the window but see nothing but blur. Phinney throws me a handful of tissues.

"I'll make it up to them. When I grow up and have kids, I'll let Mom and Dad and my sisters and Carson all live with me so I can take care of them. And we'll get new dogs."

After a long silence, Phinney makes a suggestion. "You better buy a big house."

I laugh and grab my middle as I gasp in pain.

"You okay?"

"Oh, just a few bruised ribs, scraped shoulder, and damaged hip. That's all."

Phinney comes over and hugs my head and then punches my arm.

"Ow!"

"What happened to your arm anyway?" Phinney asked.

"Bike accident at thirty miles per hour in the dark."

"Hmm. So much for basketball."

THE GUYS STOP by after school Monday to sign my cast.

Jordan checks out my face. It got cut up pretty good the night of the fire. When the police car slammed into Dad's car, it slid into the ditch and somehow missed me. But the barbed-wire fence I tried to climb didn't.

"You look like you've been in a fight, dude!"

"There are easier ways to miss school, you know." It's Bart. He's been standing in the corner of my hospital room and hasn't said a word until now.

I don't mention my "driving lesson" to my friends, but I tell them all about Carson's key saving my sisters. When they leave, Bart hangs around. The dark circles under his eyes are new. He talks about basketball. He paces and asks about the hospital food.

"I better let you get your beauty rest." His voice sounds small and lonely. He stands by the door longer than necessary. "Tell Carson I have a mess of keys he can have."

CHAPTER 51

We all make mistakes.
~Miss Thompson

They don't keep people in the hospital very long. A couple of days and they send you home, even when there's no home to go to. My parents rent a small, furnished house belonging to a retired couple wintering in Arizona.

Today is my first day "home." Carson hasn't left my side.

"I-I-I will take care of you."

He hands me a deck of Go Fish cards. "Take these."

When I reach for them, I grit my teeth. "Ahhh! My arm's killing me."

"*Mom!*" Carson yells. "Something's killing Rourke!"

"No, Carson." I chuckle. "I mean my arm hurts. It's just a saying. No one's killing me."

He walks across the small room, sits in a rocking chair, and stares at me. It's hard to tell what he's thinking.

"Don't you want to play cards?" I ask.

"They're killing you. I want to look at my stickers."

Tears spring to my eyes. His stickers are gone. I give myself some time, swallowing back guilt. "Carson. Let's order some stickers. Go get your tablet."

Miss Thompson stops in. She talks. I can't. The sound of her voice opens the floodgates. She asks questions and tries to convince me we all make mistakes. Finally, I manage two strangled words. "He's gone."

She nods, and tears fill her eyes. I close mine. It's still so painful. How can I miss someone who was never really there?

For weeks before the fire, I'd been meeting with Miss Thompson again so she could help me cope with Carson and Grace and get over Sam, but she said it wasn't enough. She wanted me to get professional help.

"I'll start seeing someone. With my parents."

When I open my eyes she's gone.

On my second day home, I wake from a nap in the recliner and Grace is kneeling next to me.

"Rourke, I was so afraid when I heard about the fire." She knows about fires. She takes my hand. "I'm sorry."

Her skin is warm and soothing. I lean my forehead against hers and manage a broken whisper. "I'm sorry for you, too."

Her forehead wrinkles. "Why?"

"You lost your mom, your home. You're poor."

She whimpers and I wipe her tears with my thumb.

"I'm not poor. We just don't have much money. I have Dad and Avery. And decent hunting skills." She smiles at this. "And you."

I mop my eyes with the back of my hand. My nose is a dripping mess. How does she stay so strong with all the junk that's happened to her?

"There are things you can learn from people who have problems, from those who are different," Grace says.

Our eyes lock for a moment before she kisses my wet cheek.

CHAPTER 52

Untangling the worry knot is messy.
~Rourke

I ask Dad to drive me to our burned house. Not much was saved, and Dad's car is toast, but we still have Mom's vintage van to get us around. As I climb in, I notice dog hair on the seat and choke back tears.

We sit in the van and stare at the charred walls and what's left of the garage. And cry.

"I messed up, Dad."

He reaches over and takes my hand. "There's plenty of blame to go around, Rourke. We put too much on you and weren't paying attention to how it was affecting you."

We sit for a few minutes, remembering. This is the place my parents brought my baby sisters home from the hospital. It's where I scribbled red ink on Mom's new wallpaper. I was three, and as soon as she got done lecturing me, I took crayons and drew some more on it.

My bedroom is gone, the seashells I collected with Grandma in Florida, my organized baseball cards. Hank. Beulah. Carson's stickers.

I would never find out if the Twinkies I stored under my bed really last twenty years. Mrs. Likens, my fifth-grade teacher, said they had enough preservatives to last that long. I used my allowance to buy some to see if she was right. I only had eighteen years left before I knew for sure.

My plastic snake collection is gone, too. I loved putting them in my sisters' beds and in the bathtub faucet so when Mom turned the water on, she'd scream bloody murder.

"Everything's gone," I whisper.

"We had too much stuff. In fact, I had so much junk in front of our basement window, I'm shocked the firemen even found it to get the girls out." His voice cracks.

Dad and I get out of the van and stand where the front door used to be. "How did Carson get out?" I ask.

"We have no idea. It's like someone carried him right through the walls. It's a miracle."

I think about that for a minute as I push my foot around in the ashes. Something shiny catches my eye, and I stoop to pick eight keys out of the soot.

"Maybe Carson can start a new collection." I smile at Dad through the blur.

"It's time to go."

Mom and Dad drive me once a week to see Dr. Miller, who has a counseling practice a half-hour away in Brookton.

At the first session we discussed my pretend friend. It was weird having my parents listen to me talk about Sam.

"At first it wasn't a big deal," I explained. "Then it became an obsession. Having someone to help me cope became a need. This sounds nuts, but I had entire conversations with him."

"Did it help?" asks Dr. Miller.

"Well, it helped calm me down...at least sometimes. Other times, the whole idea of pretending made me sick, like I was slipping away. That's when the nightmares began. I couldn't stop worrying about stuff like grades and fitting in at school, and Carson, and this homeless girl I like. But the worst was worrying about myself."

Today when we arrive, Dr. Miller asks about Carson.

I stare off and find my eyes settling on a photo on Dr. Miller's desk.

"Carson does stuff that makes me sad. Mom and Dad say he won't ever be able to live on his own. Maybe when I'm older all this won't bother me so much. But right now it does, because I'm looking forward to stuff he's never going to be able to do." My voice fades. The lump in my throat grows. "I feel guilty. And worry that it's going to always be this way."

Dr. Miller waits.

I take a deep breath and let it out. "The main thing is"—my voice is shaky—"I'm scared." I glance at my parents. They're watching the floor.

"Scared of what Carson's going to do next. Today, tomorrow, next year. Always waiting for the next time he's going to have a seizure or get hurt or be bullied or run away and never come back. And I'm freaked about what will happen to him when Mom and Dad aren't around anymore." Whispering is the best I can do.

"You mean who will take care of him?"

That's it. Right there. My eyes are flooded, my nose is dripping, and breathing is hard. "Because...I don't know how to take care of him and be happy at the same time."

After a miserable minute, I mop my face and straighten up. Mom has a tight hold on the tissue box in her lap. Dad is leaning forward, staring at the floor with his hands clasped so tight his knuckles are white.

Dr. Miller continues. "This is part of why you're here. To talk about all this and make plans. Anything else?"

"I don't know where to go to escape from worrying and now the guilt over the fire. It was my fault. I left them alone."

As Dr. Miller begins to speak again, I have trouble focusing on his words. His desk photo distracts me.

"Rourke, you care about others and that's wonderful. But there's a cost to caring. Your symptoms are similar to PTSD—post-traumatic stress disorder—and a secondary disorder called compassion fatigue, or sometimes simply called 'burnout.' We can become emotionally drained or think we have to do something to prevent or stop bad things from happening. A brother like you, who has an enormous capacity for feeling, is sometimes at a higher risk of fear and pain because you care so much. Nightmares and worry are not uncommon. Coping strategies vary from person to person."

So many words. PTSD, compassion fatigue, burnout.

The floor in the office has a familiar pattern. I trace it with my eyes. What is that shape?

Dr. Miller continues. "You coped by creating an imaginary friend to talk to. Someone you could trust with your feelings."

"Rourke? Rourke. Did you hear me?"

I look up.

"Do you know who Sam really was?"

I shrug and look at the picture on his desk again. It's Dr. Miller with his arm around a boy wearing a Superman cape. And the pattern on the floor? It's a keyhole.

Dad's keys jingle in his pocket.

Dr. Miller is still talking. "Sam was *you*. You counseled yourself by giving yourself Sam. He was your own best advice. In fact—"

"Keys!"

My outburst halts Dr. Miller's comments.

"He had the key!" I call out.

Dr. Miller's bushy eyebrows go up.

I stop to gulp in air. "All this time...I was worried about how Carson would make his way because I thought he couldn't do anything for himself. I'm wrong! Carson does stuff that makes no sense to me but works for him. His key collection... I thought it was so useless. It included the key that saved my sisters! And Carson somehow knew about Sam. It's like he has a super sense about stuff."

"My brother shouldn't be just wearing superhero shirts. He should be wearing the cape too! Just like this guy." I poke at the boy in the photo before walking out the door.

"DR. MILLER TOLD your father and me that life shouldn't revolve around Carson," Mom explains. "It's not going to be easy but we'll all try."

Dad says, "I want to spend more time with you. I'll figure out a schedule so we can do that. And we don't expect you to take care of Carson when he's older. There are lots of services to help him find a job and support his independence."

But I still have to figure out how not to worry. I found an online group called Indiana SIBS where I talk with other kids who have siblings with challenges. A girl in the group talks about acceptance as a way to overcome worry. I'm trying hard to take her advice. As I pin what she said on my bulletin board, Phinney comes into my room and reads it:

*Today I can't rid the world of every problem but I can **accept** differences, **do** what I can to make the world better, and **choose** to be happy.*

I tell Phinney about Sam. He looks at me real hard. "You don't need to imagine someone else to fix your world. You have it right in here." Phinney pokes at my chest. "And if that doesn't do it, give me a call."

Good ol' Phinney. He has often told me he wishes he had a brother. I guess we're all wishing for something we don't have.

The Salzmanns have shown me how to stop dwelling on stuff I can't change. They invited our family to their backyard for the dedication of the statue Mr. Salzmann carved of his daughter. The details of her face and hands are amazing. The way the Salzmann family has turned a horrible loss into helping others gives me hope for myself.

CHAPTER 53

The worst part about the fire was that my stickers were burned.
~Carson

I'm in no mood to celebrate my birthday, but Mom told me, "you only become a teenager once." Monica calls and tries to convince me I should have a girl-boy party, but I choose paintball.

Mom doesn't like the idea. "Shooting your friends with paintballs? You have to be careful with your arm, Rourke."

"It's just a game, Angela, and Rourke's cast is hard as a rock." Dad is more excited than me about this. When he was young, there was probably no money for fun stuff like paintball.

I invite Phinney, Bart, Justin, and Too Tall to my paintball party.

"Cool!" Bart says. "I always wondered what they used this old warehouse for!" It's hard to impress Bart, so he must like this.

"Bart, you haven't had a paintball birthday party before?"

"Are you kidding? I haven't ever had any kind of a birthday party."

He sees the doubt in my eyes and shrugs. "Mom isn't so good at planning."

A year ago, Bart would have been the last person on my invitation list. But ever since his party, he's different.

Dad plays so we have three on three.

"Ouch!" Dad yells and laughs at the same time.

"I know. It kind of stings!" says Justin.

Mom and my sisters watch. Carson didn't come, because he's playing catch with Matt, his community buddy. I bet Matt hears a lot about stickers.

After the paintball "war" we go to Tony's Pizza.

"The guys got together and made you this," Bart announces.

It's weird knowing Phinney and Bart are here together and that they worked on a gift together. Bart hands me a cardboard box with a green bow taped to it. "Best gift ever right here!"

The guys laugh.

"I'm a little afraid to open it to be honest!"

Under all the shredded newspaper I find a notebook.

"We know your English journal burned up so we got you a new one," Justin says.

"What's all this stuff?" I lift a stack of papers out of the box as the guys howl.

Bart says, "Oh, that's the stuff worth a million bucks! The entire English class was willing to give up their stash of Monica poems so you could start a collection of your own!"

Too Tall hands me a big yellow envelope that smells like someone doused it with a gallon of perfume. "You can glue her poems into the notebook and glue *this* onto the cover." The guys all snicker.

I slide out a huge colored photo of Monica all nuzzled on my shoulder at the school dance. My face heats up and the guys can't stop laughing. The photo is signed with lipstick. *All my love, Monica*

Bart smirks. "I've decided you can have Monica."

Eva asks, "Is this Marilyn Monroe's sister?" Her comment brings the house down.

"I want cake and ice cream," Eva yells from the backseat on

the way home. Lucy chimes in and pretty soon all of us are chanting, "I scream, you scream, we all scream for ice cream!"

Gramps meets us at the house. It's sad to see him alone. Just before I'm ready to blow out the candles on the leaning-tower-of-cake Mom baked, the doorbell rings.

"Surprise!"

It's Grace and her father. Mr. Salzmann and Peter come through the door, too.

After making a wish, I blow out my thirteen candles. As Mom hands out cake and ice cream, Carson and Matt arrive.

"H-h-h-appy birthday, Rourkey."

The pint-sized kitchen is packed, but no one minds.

Mom and Dad give me a "new" used bike. "You should be happy I was along, Rourke. Your dad wanted to get one like he had when he was your age; it weighed about fifty pounds and had only one speed," giggles Mom.

"Yes. Slow!" adds Dad.

Mr. Salzmann gives me a new pair of binoculars. "A true neighborhood watchman needs some binoculars."

I bite my lip. "Thank you."

I was so wrong about this man. I can add him to the growing list of other people I misjudged. Grace. Carson. Bart.

Peter hands Carson a bag. "I know it's Rourke's birthday, but I brought you a present too. Here's a bunch of fish lures. I thought you could start a new collection, and then you and I can use them to go fishing again."

"Again?" asks Mom.

"Carson and I are buds. We've gone fishing in the little pond a few times."

Peter and Carson have been fishing together? My entire family stares at Peter and then Carson and back to Peter again, attempting to process this unlikely friendship.

Dad is the first one who finds his voice. "Terrific, Peter! I love to fish. Maybe I'll join you and Carson sometime."

Lucy brings us back to a party mood. "Eva and I picked out our favorite flavors of jellybeans for you!"

"Yeah," Eva chimes in. "If you want, we can help you eat them!"

Gramps presents me with a picture of Hank and Beulah.

"Thank you, Gramps." I put the picture down before my emotions take over.

Carson hands me an envelope with stickers all over it.

"Bro! you gave up stickers for my card?" As I open it, something slips out and spins to a stop on the kitchen table.

I stare in disbelief at my wooden knot necklace. "Where did... I thought the fire..."

Carson interrupts my stammering, "I got mad when you took my keys, so I stole this w-w-wooden thing."

I exchange looks with Grace whose eyes are brimming with tears.

"Y-y-your friend, Sam, told me to give it back."

Now I'm the one with tears.

Before I can even begin to process what he just said, Carson grabs the envelope and reads what he wrote in his card. "The fire chief is giving me an award for helping him use my key to open the door during the fire. I want you to bring me to get my award. Happy Birthday to the best brother. Love, Carson"

I swallow hard, and with a cracked voice I finally speak. "You got it bro! I wouldn't miss it!" Carson's eyes are on the floor. I want to hug him, but he wouldn't like it.

"Our present is an announcement!" Grace's voice is bouncing.

"I've been offered a job in Chicago," Grace's dad says.

Oh no. She's moving.

"But there's been enough change in our lives the past year. So, we've decided to stay in Hazard."

I squeeze my eyes shut in relief.

"I've had an offer to join the law firm of Adams and Meyer right here in town. We just leased a townhouse about a mile from here."

Wow. That candle wish thing works fast!

"And the best part is Avery gets to come and live with us again!" Grace hops up and down and squeals.

"So you'll be around to go to the movie on Saturday?" I give her a look to show I haven't forgotten.

"Only if there's popcorn with extra butter."

I want to wrap my arms around her. But I just sigh a huge sigh and smile. Her eyes sparkle back at me, making it a perfect thirteenth birthday.

CHAPTER 54

Carson's treasures are priceless.
~Rourke

When I get home from school I hear music coming from the room I share with Carson so I wander in. He's sitting cross-legged on the floor wearing his newest Superman shirt and sunglasses. The fire chief's medal hangs from his neck. An old phone book is on his lap. The eight keys I found are on the windowsill. Several erasers are lined up along the rug. It's a new collection.

Without looking up at me, he says, "What?"

"Oh, nothin'. Just thought I'd come and say hi."

"Well, then say it."

"Hi, Carson." I can't help but smile.

He begins numbering the pages of the new notebook I bought him. "Help me." It's more of an expectation than a demand.

"What should I do?"

"Hold the pages open."

The song "Don't Stop Believin'" is playing. "What happened to 'Red Solo Cup'?"

"It burned up."

I fight the sadness that still sits inside me. How can it bother me so much and not faze him?

My eyes settle on the framed picture on the dresser of

Carson shaking the fire chief's hand. I don't remember being more proud than I was that day. I wasted so much energy on what he lacked and never saw what he had. Never saw his invisible "cape."

And Sam? Carson knew about him? He probably overheard me talking to him.

After about twenty pages of numbering I kneel beside him. "You know, Carson, if they lined up all the kids in Hazard and I got to choose one to be my LINK, you know who I'd pick?"

There's a long pause before he stops writing and stares at my chest as if deep in thought. "Are they lined up on the fifty-yard line?"

"Of course!"

Another long pause.

"I th-think you'd pick...Annabelle."

This cracks me up. When I'm done laughing, I say, "No! *You*. I'd pick you. I'd pick Carson."

Without looking at me, he says, "I'd pick you, too," and goes back to numbering.

EPILOGUE

I haven't been in Mr. Dunphey's room for two years. It looks the same, and he's still picking things out of his beard. There are no piñatas dangling from the ceiling today. I look at the light Carson destroyed. It's been repaired of course, and no one would know it had been attacked.

It's LINK Day, and my ninth-grade homeroom class with Miss Thompson has been paired with Mr. Dunphey's seventh-graders. Grace smiles at me from where she's standing by her LINK, Ella. We are halfway through the pairings, and it's my turn.

"My name is Rourke and my LINK is Cedric Allen." I smile and walk over to Cedric and kneel beside his wheelchair. Cedric makes a sharp, cawing sound, and his eyes dance with joy. I reach out to high five him, and his twisted hand makes a shaky attempt to meet mine.

A few weeks ago when we were filling out our LINK profiles I wrote a note on mine, asking if there were any seventh graders who had special challenges. Miss Thompson told me about Cedric.

Cedric was born with cerebral palsy. He has trouble controlling his muscles and movements. His speech is difficult to understand so he uses an electronic communication board to have a conversation.

"Can I be his LINK?"

I didn't think Miss Thompson was ever going to answer me. "Are you sure?"

Smiling, I told her, "Yes, it's fine."

And for the first time in my life, I believe it.

ACKNOWLEDGMENTS

A book is a group effort. I want to express my deepest gratitude to Holli Anderson for believing in this story. Her dependable communication, efficient editing, and positive approach made the process fun and professional. A huge shout out to the rest of the talented Immortal Works crew as well-Ashley, Ruth, Staci, Megan, and Jason-for putting all the flying parts of book production and promotion together. Their expertise and dedication to making books that matter is inspiring. A special thank you to my family for being my rock through all *my* worries! You are all extraordinary.

AUTHOR'S NOTE

This book is about what we all do at some point. Worry. *The Worry Knot* tells how it might be for an almost thirteen year-old to be entering the awkward years of middle school and be plagued with worry when he'd rather just fit in and play sports.

I started writing this story after our youngest graduated from high school. My husband and I had made it through the early years of realizing something was amiss when our son was a toddler and still wasn't speaking, when his (lack of) social skills caused him frustration and tangles with others, and when he finally received an ASD diagnosis. We were vigilant about getting him all the support he needed but we worried about him. We also worried about how his challenges affected our other children and what the future held. There's no question that challenging abilities affect families, friendships, and futures. What I didn't realize then is how those challenges would have a positive outcome. Inspiration and admiration are two words that float to the surface. The lives of those who know our son have been enriched in a way I never imagined.

This book isn't *our* family story, but I stirred up a slice of both the angst and the joy we experienced and created a new one in *The Worry Knot*. Although I wrote it for middle grade readers, who are often in the thick of the awkward years, I believe the story will resonate with all who have endured or observed circumstances beyond their control.

As an author, I write to give readers a chance to recognize

that their emotions are empowering and can lead to resiliency and change. Beyond the obvious dilemmas, *The Worry Knot*, is about finding acceptance and hope and most importantly, highlighting the notion that an individual least expected to contribute can indeed make extraordinary contributions.

DISCUSSION GUIDE

1. Rourke has an imaginary friend to help him cope with his worries. What do you do to handle your worries and concerns?

2. Has there been a time when you've imagined or longed for someone to fulfill a need?

3. Do you feel Rourke's parents put too much on him? Have you ever felt that someone (parent, teacher, etc.) has given you more responsibility than you can handle?

4. Do you know anyone who reminds you of Bart? How did he change in this story?

5. The word *misperception* means a mistaken belief about something. There are misperceptions that characters have in this story. Who has them and what are they? Have you ever formed a perception about someone and found out you were mistaken?

6. Loss is one theme in this story. Loss of dreams of having a "typical" brother and loss of a mother for Grace are examples. Can you name other losses in the book? How do these losses affect characters (in good and bad ways)?

7. Carson's key collection saves his sisters. Have you known anyone with a surprising ability? What can you do to help bring out the best in these individuals?

8. Why was LINK day so important to Rourke?

9. The word "fine" is used several times and the book concludes with a line about it. What is the significance of its use in this story? Do you sometimes use that response when things really aren't fine?

10. We often remember books by our favorite characters. Who is your favorite character in *The Worry Knot* and why?

BIBLIOGRAPHY

Listed alphabetically below are the standout selections of writings and music I have referred to and borrowed from in the construction of my novel, *The Worry Knot*.

BOOKS

Erickson, John R. *The Original Adventures Of Hank The Cowdog*. Perryton, TX: Maverick Books, 1983. Print.

Hinton, S. E. *The Outsiders*. New York City: Viking Press, 1967. Print.

Lee, Harper. *To Kill A Mockingbird*. Philadelphia: Lippincott, 1960. Print.

Glenday, Craig. Guinness Book Of Records. Vancouver: Jim Pattison Book Group, 2015. Print.

POEMS
Frost, Robert. "Nothing Gold Can Stay". As reprinted by Hinton, S. E. *The Outsiders*. New York City: Viking Press, 1967. Chapter 5. Print.

SONGS
Beatles, The. "Hey Jude." By John Lennon and Paul

McCartney. Single A-side, B-side "Revolution". London: Apple Records, 1968. Vinyl.

Diamond, Neil. "Sweet Caroline." By Neil Diamond. *Brother Love's Travelling Salvation Show*. Hollywood: Uni Records, 1969. Vinyl.

Journey. "Don't Stop Believin'." By Jonathan Cain, Steve Perry, Neal Schon. *Escape*. New York City: Columbia Records, 1981. Vinyl.

Keith, Toby. "Red Solo Cup". By Brett Beavers, Jim Beavers, Brad Warren, Brett Warren. *Clancy's Tavern*. Nashville: Show Dog-Universal Music, 2011. Digital Download.

Los del Rio. "Macarena". By Rafael Ruiz Perdigones, Antonio Romero Monge, SWK. *A Mi Me Gusta*. New York City: RCA Records, 1995. Vinyl.

Village People, "Y.M.C.A.". By Jacques Morali, Victor Willis. *Cruisin'*. New York City: Casablanca Records, 1978. Vinyl.

Television

BBC Worldwide, prod. "Dancing With The Stars". Dancing With The Stars. ABC, CBS Television City, Los Angeles. 1 June 2005 – present.

Film

Happy Feet. Dir. George Miller. Perf. Elijah Wood, Robin Williams. Warner Bros. Pictures, 2006. Film.

ABOUT THE AUTHOR

MARY BLECKWEHL is the author of *The Birthday Cookbook* for children as well as three award-winning picture books, *Henry you're late AGAIN! Henry you're hungry AGAIN?* and *Claire's Hair*. As a writer she uses words to challenge readers to not just imagine a better world but to take action to make it so. Bleckwehl grew up in a big farm family in Iowa with few books but many experiences that are the foundation of her writing. In school, she learned that both magic and knowledge blossomed in words and enthusiastically grabbed every opportunity to read. She now lives in Minnesota where she's been a teacher, an advocate of different abilities, and juggles her love of writing with life's many joys. Bleckwehl and her husband have three children, two grandchildren, and a mammoth goldendoodle named Sadie.

This has been an
Immortal Production